MAKE DUST OUR PAPER

A NOVEL

JOSEPH M. REYNOLDS

ANAPHORA LITERARY PRESS

BROWNSVILLE, TEXAS

Anaphora Literary Press
1898 Athens Street
Brownsville, TX 78520
https://anaphoraliterary.com

Book design by Anna Faktorovich, Ph.D.

Printed in the United States of America, United Kingdom and in Australia on acid-free paper.

Published in 2017 by Anaphora Literary Press

Make Dust Our Paper: A Novel
Joseph M. Reynolds—1st edition.

Library of Congress Control Number: 2017905789

Library Cataloging Information

Reynolds, Joseph M., 1981-, author.
Make dust our paper: A novel / Joseph M. Reynolds
122 p. ; 9 in.
ISBN 978-1-68114-335-4 (softcover : alk. paper)
ISBN 978-1-68114-336-1 (hardcover : alk. paper)
ISBN 978-1-68114-337-8 (e-book)
1. Fiction—Literary. 2. Philosophy—Movements—Existentialism.
3. Philosophy—Movements—Idealism. I. Title.
PN3311-3503: Literature: Prose fiction
813: American fiction in English

MAKE DUST OUR PAPER

A NOVEL

JOSEPH M. REYNOLDS

Let's talk of graves, of worms, or epitaphs;
Make dust our paper and with rainy eyes
Write sorrow on the bosom of the earth,
Let's choose executors and talk of wills;
And yet not so, for what can we bequeath
Save our deposed bodies to the ground?
Our lands, our lives and all are Bolingbroke's,
And nothing can we call our own but death
And that small model of the barren earth
Which serves as paste and cover to our bones.
For God's sake, let us sit upon the ground
And tell sad stories of the death of kings.

—*Richard II*

SEPTEMBER 3, 1997

As seemingly far too many people had done before him, freshman John Carrigan sat pensively in a lecture hall at that grand university in New Haven on September 3, 1997. And he was particularly alert as he listened to his Modern Political Thought professor tell one of his favorite stories—"On November 22, 1963, in the same hour that President Kennedy was pronounced dead at Parkland Memorial Hospital in Dallas, Sir Laurence Olivier was playing Hamlet at the Old Vic in London. Upon hearing of the young President's untimely demise during a costume change, Olivier interrupted the performance during the third scene of the second act, and demanded that the orchestra play the 'Star Spangled Banner.' The audience stood with Olivier, and with hands pressing against hearts, many wept solemnly."

Carrigan quickly opened his notebook and found the first blank page. Then, in large capital letters, he wrote a question—***WILL THEY INTERRUPT "HAMLET" WHEN I DIE?***

There were some things that were true about John Carrigan—he was a genius and everybody said so. He had the soul and wit of a poet and everybody noticed. He had a heart that was receptive enough to break at a moment's warning, and the verve to be either purely great or wretchedly mean or disappointing, depending on the moment. And he had a penchant for noticing the wrong thing about things.

This is a story that purports to be about a year—not a calendar year, but more accurately, an academic one—John Carrigan's senior year to be exact, which began on September 1, 2000 and ended in the first week of May 2001—the final year of philosophy as Carrigan preferred calling it. It's true that very many people—both spectacular and shockingly mundane alike—had spent their college years in New Haven before Carrigan did, and this essentially represented Carrigan's chief dilemma in his final academic year—a lot of people had already died for all of the causes worth dying for. Guns had gone muffled and silent. Heartbeats had slowed to a frighteningly contented and calm sort of rhythm. The last decent literary age was over; the next one not yet in sight, and worse, not even yet yearned for. The economy ostensibly worked. Love seemed easy and always within reach. Sports made sense. Trains showed up on time. Every movie that came out was satisfactory to its intended audience. War was a memory. Peace was non-philosophical. Music was good again, but not great. And with the tepid acceptance of the Good Friday agreements a few years before, quiet had come to even the north of Ireland. The questions of the age had not been settled, but had instead been forgotten; lost in the malaise of store bought joy, practical use degrees, and timeshare vacations. It was an age of too little despair, and not enough righteousness. No, it seemed quite unlikely that *Hamlet* would be interrupted when Carrigan came to die.

Now, some footnotes are appropriate here. First, while it seems unfortunate, the story of a year is never only about the year it chronicles. There is a kind of human frailty and discontent that makes any year's narrative so inherently but messily linked to vignettes of years that came before it—many of which the narrative's featured players weren't even alive for, and far too many of which taking place on terrains that they will never step foot on, or worse, terrains that no longer exist. And it isn't only the past that distorts the story of a year; the vanity of thoughts of years to come, the insidiousness of planning, the capricious and liminal nature of hope, the desperate voyeurism into one's own future, steal the temporal year from us as well.

As the millennium changed, Carrigan had yet to solve these issues, and so the story of his final year of philosophy, or so he thought at least, becomes, by nature, the story of several others—some shadowy, some confusing, some alienating, and many that seem asymmetrical. But journalistic sequencing isn't truth. Narrative timelines aren't truth. And well, truth isn't even truth, in the sense that it is dormant and worthless without interpretation, and as soon as we interpret, we lose our unity—and rightly so; we are nothing if not distinctly troubled in our own unique ways—nothing if not particularly biased by our own debilitating experiences and the depravity that ensues.

What we are left with is a rich and fascinating muddle of context; a maze of qualification and influence that both distorts and, somewhere inside its intricate, openly deceitful kaleidoscope holds the illuminating answers to our confusion. There's a romance in all that searching—a kind of William Blake-like peace in the wild things that comes as strangely and as quickly as it goes, and so we believe in it even when our failure to see it breaks us down. Irascibility is romance.

And so, in proper form, this, like the story of any year, is a story appropriately told in carefully selected and assiduously manipulated vignettes. Accordingly, you will likely find many of these vignettes entertaining, many heartbreaking, and still more that are tedious and disenfranchising. This narrative makes one strident and correctly nondescript promise—John Carrigan is a young man worth knowing.

Maybe when our vignettes move closer together and seem to display a kind of causal relationship towards one another, we can say we have something approaching a life instead of a series of artistically manipulated episodes of memory, but who is really to say which one of these options is better anyway?

MAY 15, 1991

John Carrigan was born on New Year's Day and spent the rest of his life looking over his shoulder to see if anyone was catching up. He always wanted to go to Princeton. And he always wanted to drop out before he was finished. And on this day he took his first broad step towards Scott Fitzgerald's playground of spires and gargoyles.

Three months later he would complete the dyad of childhood Renaissance accomplishment at the Little League World Series, but today he sat on the stage in the auditorium of the Capitol Hilton in Washington, DC, and he waited solemnly for the finals of the National Spelling Bee to commence. He wore the standard over-sized white golf shirt, and the cardboard placard with his name and his sponsor newspaper, *The New Haven Register*, dangled around his neck as he leaned forward with heavy eyes, his sunken head suspended just above his knees. Most of the kids on the stage were nervous, and many of them were obnoxious, but 12-year-old John Carrigan was the only one who was bored. He had fierce green eyes and brown hair. He was (it goes somewhat without saying) a damned handsome kid, but normal would've been good enough to stand out on this scaffold. He was surrounded by a bevy of kids with uneven haircuts and pants that were too tight and too short and with parents who didn't know enough or didn't care enough to teach their kids about such things and with lives too secluded to figure it out on their own. The love affairs that had produced such children were not the products of tragic melancholy or even whimsical mistake that burns itself out into either resentment or solace over time, but instead were the direct effects of an efficient understanding of expediency, duty, and societal ceremony, and Carrigan pitied the ideas that brought their nativities, and believed, at 12, that he would always be happy because he valued the fact that he was so sad, so often.

John Carrigan's khaki pants hung gently over the shoe-tops of his untied Adidas Superstars—the white shell-tops with the three black stripes up the side. He kept them untied to make sure that he always had something to do, or at least to avoid giving the impression that his mind was ever solely focused on a competition to arrange letters in their right and proper order. For the same reason, he occupied himself during classes at school by writing the states down in his notebook, and trying to name every Red Sox leftfielder since 1920.

The truth was, Johnny Carrigan really did like the Spelling Bee, admired and revered and found romantic the pure and natural and untaught, genius aspect of being really good at it, but he despised the fact that no one else really seemed to view it exactly the same way—even then despised that the trophy seemed to be some sort of monument to study and self-denial and discipline, rather than an emblem of a mind that was just a bit more divinely chosen than the rest. He had a kind of lustful and even sordid fascination for qualities that one possessed without trying or training; it was an example of human difference, of random human difference not allocated by geography or heredity or nepotistic or convivial favor. There was a divinity and a romance in that for Carrigan, and an acknowledgement of a remnant of the untouched in a loathsome and discovered world. And so he sat sullen and restless and hungry, and he waited his turn to lose at a contest that he didn't even respect, and he wondered if there would ever be another pick-up basketball game at the park back home, or if the one he was missing today was the last one ever to be like it and he was forsaking that part of his life to sit next to a kid who smelled funny and who wouldn't smile or talk to him. On the other side sat one of those angry and defiant handicapped kids, who was making his already greasy brown hair sweaty at the tips by constantly driving in circles around the other contestants and pulling up his front wheels so as to emphasize the things he could do that the others could not, as opposed to the reverse.

And then they called his name, and his eyes burned a hole through the moderator's forehead as he grabbed the microphone and let a sly smile sheepishly fade across his weary, 12-year-old, too-handsome face.

The word was "ascetic;" a rather easy word for the national finals, but Carrigan barely even heard it. He was ready to manufacture whatever word they gave him into a faint but ruminating aura of injustice, or at least disavowal of the enterprise. He didn't ask for the word to be repeated, didn't ask for it in a sentence, didn't ask if there were alternate pronunciations; his smile had turned deep and menacing as he was ready to make his exit. He looked down with eyes closed in consternation and then looked quickly up and shot a squinty Clint Eastwood-as-Josey Wales-type stare not at the moderator, but at the kid next in line for the microphone. He sputtered out a whirling, confusing, seemingly dyslexic maze of letters—he made sure to give the correct letters but arrange them in the wrong order. He so confused the judges that they actually paused in disbelief before dinging their tiny bell of ignominy. As the ring still echoed in the ballroom, Carrigan had already knocked over his chair (his adrenaline was pumping so he covered it consciously with clangorous noise) and made it to the hotel lobby. He bummed a cigarette, took one puff and flicked it away, hiding his nauseated cough until he was outside, and caught a blue-line Metro train with his placard still dangling around a neck that seemed too burdened for his age—all before his mother could bring herself to stand up from her chair.

Emily Mary Carrigan found her son in their hotel room watching the contest on television and rooting, with absolute sincerity, for the kids he had walked out on. He had spelled all the words and listed them on a loose-leaf piece of paper (he needed proof of something), with the idea that anything could be transubstantiated if you really believed enough. As the winner spelled the last word, Carrigan looked innocently into his mother's unyielding green eyes and asked, with total innocence, if it would be okay for them to leave now. It was the first words they had spoken since Carrigan had kissed her proud cheek that morning as he was about to mount the stage. Anticipatory remorse had prevented him from looking into her green eyes then, but he stared deeply and almost longingly into them now. Emily Mary Carrigan stepped into the bathroom and cried a deep-throated cry of both pride and terror for a world she knew could never be big enough for John, her third-born son and fourth child of seven in all.

DECEMBER 25, 1913

Kiernan Carrigan's blue eyes were a pure blue, the last pure set in the family. America had assimilated or watered down or made more rich—depending on who you were speaking of—the purity of the blue in every Carrigan since. But on Christmas Morning, 1913, Kiernan's eyes shone fierce in the Portrush mist. He was 21 years old, the oldest of seven, with history assembled both before and after him. Kiernan always kept the same expression, which did him no disservice, for it held so many emotions. He scowled and smiled at once, questioning the authenticity of any claim, but loving the discourse of the hunt. He scowled because he believed in many things, believed in them deeply, and he would not tolerate any affront to their esteem. He squinted through deep gray smoke, picking up his head as he removed the cigarette exquisitely from his mouth, almost doubting the veracity of the smoke itself. He never drank because he was in love with his wit. And his love was loyal and unwavering. He would not bear obscuring its grace even temporarily, even in indiscriminate increments, even in the joy of revelry or celebration or well-earned ecstasy. He loved all the things that only he was able to see, and he never wanted to miss a moment. It was why he believed so deeply; his impenetrable mind would never lead him astray.

His back leaned against the outside of the wooden front door that served as the only entrance to the symmetrical brick house. As the bells rang 6, Kiernan's gray smoke was dwarfed by the churning black smoke of the chimney above. He opened the door and yelled in a loving but distant greeting, put out his cigarette, and started heading north. His mother helplessly called to her eldest son, but tempered her urgency, unable to muster any dissent to the desire at hand. He would come back.

The rain grew steady, but Kiernan did not cower, only increased his pace to meet the ferocity of his obstacle—his was a nature wonderfully in rhythm with God's. His relationship with the Divine was one of poetic give and take; he grew strong as the world grew rough, and relaxed in step (and in attendance at Mass) with the coming of the breeze. His hair was so black it refracted all glints of color. It never darkened his person but attracted the luminous rays that fight against the perpetual Irish shadow. And the rain served only to deepen his black austerity, which, set against the blue ferocity of his eyes, made him look nothing short of idyllic—with Kiernan, one had to use the ubiquitous descriptors; they were made for him after all, or that is to say, he was the kind of man that taught people what they meant.

He rounded the corner thinking of Midnight Mass and what a good writer Father Banville could have been (could one still be a great writer if his efforts breathe and die only in the pulpits?) and passed two British sentries who were armed and stationed outside of a makeshift military office that had been converted from an old Catholic church that the English had bankrupted with the sort of backhanded banality of presence that fostered absolute intimidation. Kiernan looked sharply into their eyes with perfect Irish sanctity; he hated Britain but not the British. At least one of them was desperate; one of them always looked back into Kiernan's eyes. It was now Christmas in every inch of the Western World.

Kiernan's delight in theoretical psychology was trumped by inexpressible anxiety as the bells rang 7. He was close, and Christ, he would know what to do when he got there. He knocked with sustained fervor and he knew she would definitely be the one to answer. He remembered what she looked like immediately, with a rush of knowing surprise that only true and continuously mounting love provides. He could see by the shrouded tears adding eloquent perspective to her still-innocent smile that she had received the letters in time, which was of no consequence, for he had remembered every syllable and was prepared to recite them as he held her, but now instead, he just held her. He was in love before popular music or motion picture would make him an ideal. He was unequivocally the best writer in the history of the Carrigans, but he never published a word. He didn't have to. He never compromised himself. He didn't have to. He wouldn't be the last righteous Carrigan, whatever that meant, but he'd be the last happy one, or at least the last one who embraced happiness as being something worthwhile.

The train took a leisurely southeast path, and they arrived at Dublin's Connolly Station at 9:29 am. They took a left into the bustling Christmas grandeur of O'Connell Street, where no one seemed to be fighting about whose Christ belonged in Ireland, or at least they were distracted by reunion or gift receiving or whiskey. Kiernan took her hand and guided her into St. Mary's Cathedral on Marlborough in the time when a man like Kiernan would attend both the Midnight Mass and the morning service—a more longing time, if not a more mournful time.

He knelt for the solemn intersession, and when his head rose, he noticed for the first time that his Portrush neighbor, Ulsterman Colin McGirn, who had laughed inappropriately when they were boys and now had a smile made grim by a chipped tooth, sat in a pew across the aisle on his left, and their heads nodded in a kind of final union; it was too late not to be friends. It was today. They were 21 together.

McGirn had been a clumsy footballer, and Kiernan thought now only of the time that Colin had uproariously mounted his back and embraced his shoulders when Kiernan's bending left-footed kick had beaten Eamen Feeney, and the team of Carrigan and McGirn had become the first pair to ever defeat the Feeney twins at anything. It was his only shared memory—they went to different schools, just as they usually went to different churches.

Kiernan blessed himself sanguinely and slowly, but said no act of contrition. He rose, and they walked directly out. He stopped abruptly—his pristine, suddenly too-handsome face was dampening under the frigid mist, and he told her he loved her for the first time that day.

He quickly cut across to the other side of the spire and read with reverie about what would play next at the Abbey. It was *Heartbreak House*. He liked Shaw. He started to think desperately of all of the things he liked.

He crossed the Liffey on the Trinity side, and saw the tourists marveling at the smooth, humming current, and the kaleidoscope of light that it refracted. He didn't stop; he could bear no requiem.

He and Audrey (he had finally begun calling her by name) walked past that proud Goldsmith statue and through Trinity's gates and onto the rough cobblestone. They turned left at the edge of the green and entered Botany Bay—Kiernan had a third-floor dorm room, and he wanted to collect some of his things. Audrey half-sat and half-lay on his bed and absently looked out of the window that overlooked the courtyard. Her hair was as deep and black as the far side of the Liffey in the midnight hour, and her green eyes were always inviting, and never opaque. She moved with unconscious agility and Kiernan remembered a 12-year-old Audrey kicking a football against the retaining wall on Astor when none of the boys would kick it with her. She joked easily, and tugged playfully at the tail of his coat as he rummaged through his desk with his back facing her. She read Marlowe and Emerson (no one Irish—Ireland was a birthplace for her, not an aspiration, and she found subtle ways to prepare for the leaving), and had a pocket Keats in her fashionable grey overcoat with the upturned collar.

Now he felt contrite—*Oh my God, I am heartily sorry for having offended thee*...he stopped; it wasn't God's forgiveness that he needed. He found an inscribed copy of *Dorian Gray* and tucked it in his coat—this had been Wilde's room (or maybe they had lied to him about that)—and he stuffed some letters and trinkets and coins into his pockets. He then removed the ring from one of his internal pockets, and locked it in his desk. Why should she have to know what they had lost? Why should he poison the marriage she would come to with thoughts of what had been washed away? "God damn it all," he thought. He didn't even have time to decide if he was right or not.

They stood by the quiet pond closest to the southern entrance to St. Stephen's Green. Little children pushed and shouted to each other with loosened tiny neckties that signified the escape from Mass. Kiernan kissed Audrey voraciously, but not necessarily hurriedly. He then stood with hands in pockets, and moved from under the archway to the open air. The forgettable McGirn had one truly worldly talent; Kiernan was dead before Audrey heard the shot.

It was so cold that his blood ran nowhere; just froze in place in a darkening pool behind his head, already staining the pavement through to a seeming other side. Audrey cried and then stopped. She ran in a circle, and then stopped. She knelt and took the keys from his coat pocket. She ascended the Botany Bay stairs. She made the sign of the cross. She fell into a deep and dreamless sleep in Kiernan's bed. It was a final time of isolated and insulated reverence before the dean came to take the keys back and that aspirational life to be lived somewhere else would have to begin, years before it was supposed to; years before she wanted to leave a place that she loved but resented, like a sibling that annoys or a refreshing rain that leaves puddles and quasi-permanent stains.

JANUARY 26, 1988

It was the first airplane ride that nine-year-old John Carrigan had taken since his initial trip from Dublin to America when he was an infant. But he didn't remember that one. So for all intents and purposes, this was it; his maiden voyage through the air, and he distrusted it and felt bullied by its acceptance, as if somehow something only practiced for an infinitesimal percentile in the history of man had suddenly become natural or commonplace, or at least not harped upon in reverence or terror.

He had been the last Carrigan born in Dublin. His mother, Emily Mary Carrigan, thought of this as she scurried her five living children to the airport. She openly mourned the fact that for John, and the two younger than him, air travel would always be juxtaposed against the reason for this trip—the burial of their father.

John had only the faintest recognition of his father as it was—Peter Carrigan had been away doing "dangerous but altogether necessary and divine things" (he couldn't remember which aunt had phrased it that way; they all seemed the same—washed wan charm in prematurely aging red faces) from the time John was six. John heard but didn't comprehend terms like IRA, and Home Rule, and Sinn Fein, and Ulstermen, and partition. All he knew about Catholics was that he was one, and that every Saturday since his last birthday he was to tell a priest about all of the less than virtuous things he had done. The Sacrament of Reconciliation they called it (his mother told him it was the most important one), and it would keep him in good favor with God, and keep his heart pure, and the gates of Heaven open. The trick wasn't to avoid sin; it was to feel genuinely bad about it when you did sin. John Carrigan could handle that, even by age eight; every time he saw tears well up in his mother's shining, enveloping, oceanic eyes he felt instantly guilty. Even if he hadn't had any part in the cause of the thing, his heart broke a little. And her eyes welled up almost daily after the day his father had departed for a green island John knew nothing of, but somehow dominated the scope of his young life. John's heart was perpetually full with sorrow for all the things he couldn't control. And he always felt bad when sadness encroached upon his atmosphere, mostly because he coveted it so eagerly and enjoyed it so cravenly. He was certainly banking some favor for the next world.

Every week at confession, he would confess the same sins—foul language, tempestuous anger directed at a sibling, selfishness. And every week Father Lenihan would ask him the same question.

"Do you promise not to do it again, lad?"

"I promise to try not to, Father. I can't promise I'll be able to, or else I wouldn't be in here confessing the same sins as last week. But I will try my hardest. And I do feel bad when I screw it up."

Father Lenihan laughed every time. John Carrigan had this reconciliation thing all figured out.

All John knew about Protestants was that they were the men "who shot guns at your father for protecting his natural right to live in a homeland," that they "were the ones who threw rocks at little Catholic school girls because they had traded in their souls for the false and dead pursuit of empire" (Later, he struggled to remember which red-faced aunt had talked so pedantically, so much in campaign talking points?). John had no idea what any of this meant, but he could never forget the terminology—it was repeated, on loop, like some horrible record that grown-ups play after dinner, except this one had no music, and had no interval, and no opportunity of concluding and turning over to a more palatable track with rhythm or heartbeat.

And he learned a new term today—*bereavement.* His mother used it several times to the ticket clerk—a last second rate that airlines give in case of emergency.

"What does that word mean?"

"It means we're sad, John."

"Why do we have to be sad?"

"Because your father has died, John. And we miss him. But we're going to honor him. We're going home. And I need you to be brave and strong." Did she have to memorize these lines or did they come instinctually?

Home. Ireland. Beyond the fact that the older members of his family talked with a different lilt than he and his brothers and sisters, he had no idea what Irish was, but he knew it was a big deal. It was the word he heard most often. John had not cried yet. He hadn't really known his father in any kind of personal way, and all of the ceremony and import surrounding his death seemed like a proper source of pride; that Peter Carrigan mattered, and so in turn, his son did too. But, he hadn't been to another funeral so he couldn't really be sure if it mattered at all.

When the plane started to descend on Dublin, his mother told him to observe how green the countryside was, but her warning didn't do it justice.

"It's green Mom. But a different kind of green from home."

"Yes," Emily Carrigan said, and a wan smile escaped her lips. It was the first somewhat happy attitude John had seen in her in months. She had tried feigning it for the children from time to time, but every time she smiled, the tears consumed her eyes simultaneously. They were like some wicked external form of visible conscience that refused her the benign dignity of disguising her true emotions. It had worn on John, and he hadn't realized how much until she had been able to maintain this smile without crying for the first time.

The rest of the trip came and went like a supposedly important dream that one can only remember parts of—a maddening dream because aspects escape your recollection even as one can feel their essentiality somewhere in the bones. But he couldn't really be sure that it was important at all.

John remembered getting dressed, or that is, having his mother dress him, as he hadn't worn a real necktie before.

"Why can't I just wear the clip-on tie I usually wear for Mass?"

"Because you're going to tug at it John, and when you tug at this one, at least it won't come popping off." She was kind of a virtuoso at predicting the idiosyncratic behavior of her children.

The funeral mass was at Our Lady of Peace Parish on Merion Road in Dublin's fourth district. He couldn't name the word then, but it was irony that he was learning about. "Peace," he thought sardonically. Why was the word ironic? And he felt disgusted for reasons he couldn't express, but still he didn't cry.

The day was composed of a litany of men his father's age and older speaking to him in brogues. The women just kissed his forehead and prayed to Saint Peter. The men said things they probably shouldn't have.

"Your father was a real fighter, lad. He wouldn't give those bastards the satisfaction of crying out. They shot him like livestock in the middle of Victoria Road, and it took him a good half hour to bleed out. Not one of those animals offered him even the slightest aspect of human kindness as he lay helpless and dying in that road, bullets spent from his pistol, blood seeping through his undershirt. Be proud, lad."

It was actually the first time in days that John didn't feel proud. There was something unsettling about the violence, and it had nothing to do with his father. There was something too vivid about the violence that no amount of repentance (no matter how ardently you said your ten Hail Mary's) could expiate from your moral record, or cleanse your consciousness of. And they celebrated it, and John felt like he was witnessing a vulgarity that he was meant to be shielded from forever. He ran to the bathroom and vomited, and they all slapped him on the back and praised the fire in him. They lauded this great love he felt for a father who had lived a continent away most of the time. They laughed and sang with whiskey-infiltrated breaths, or more accurately, spoke in breaths that infiltrated their whiskey. They were passionate and compassionate. They didn't hide their sorrow and they expressed it like poets, reciting the old songs and the old verses (always intermingled with eloquent articulations of their own) with the proper amount of piety, and an obvious kind of resignation. This was what Irish was to young Carrigan—an acceptance of death; a forfeiture of this place; the hopelessness of a struggle that would still never be abandoned; a life where your most profound moments were reserved for the ending of it. Carrigan vomited again. But still he did not cry.

The most patently disturbing aspect about all of the talk of violence was that it seemed like an ardent and vulgar fiction. John's mother had told him that his father had "caught an infection" and died before the doctors could find out which infection it was; that was almost too symbolic—Peter Carrigan always running away before things got too specific or concrete. One of his sisters told him that he had been in a train accident, but she was the worst liar of the bunch, in that she was the sweetest and kindest (she earned simple words because she lived up to them assiduously, to a point that it was almost a source of derangement) person he ever knew and she coughed when she lied, as if some physical spasm of sanctity was reminding her of her venial sin and giving her one last chance to abort the expulsion of the lie's syllables. John asked her if she had bronchitis or if she was dying herself when recounting her tale. She started to cry at that, another bad liar's tip-off, as classic as it was. He made no judgment about his sister's propensity for sincerity and the physical backlash its obfuscation engendered, as he was undecided as to the worthiness of truth as a concept, and as to the nature of literality in an already less than artistic world. The one thing he could not discern, and it was the singular thing that troubled him, was whether the others themselves didn't know the truth (including his mother)—whether they were lying or being lied too, and who might actually know, and more importantly, why (more than how) they had been allowed to know.

The men who regaled John about the bullets and the blood on Victoria Road had never been seen before, not even in the grey pictures on his parent's nightstand; not even in the yellowing album of his father's that John had clandestinely and almost lasciviously looked through upon finding accidentally, while burrowing through the recesses of an ancient drawer searching for a matching sock to replace the ripped one in his hand, so he could look proper while attending some interminable recital or school play where no one would see his socks anyway. He remembered the faces there, in that album, with an eidetic and burrowing sheen, and none of these bravado-speaking, whiskey-soaked, cheerily mourning men were assembled on the yellowing pages with the hard water stains, with the corners worn as if they were constantly, if not perpetually, looked upon.

His mother cried often, but it was different than it had been; she was pretty again (he realized only by its return that her beauty had retreated for a time, and John absorbed that as a resonant sign that she had loved his father, at least in some way), and her dress sauntered around her waist flowingly as she moved with great agility and poise around the mazes of people.

Carrigan cried for the first time that April. He was back home in New Haven, and it was opening day of the Little League baseball season. He came up to bat third in the bottom of the first inning. Robby St. John was on the mound, and grooved the first pitch, dead straight and heading towards the inside corner. Carrigan deftly turned on it and homered off the green scoreboard in left field of Basset Park, already marred by generations of homerun balls from aspirational boys, most of whom went nowhere. The entire town was there; opening day was accompanied by a parade and formal introductions of all of the players, and a raucous cheer erupted when Carrigan's homerun reverberated off that old metal placard of wistful and unfulfilled glory. It was his first home run, and he sprinted around the bases pumping his fist with determination, but never able to conceal the broad grin that enveloped his entire face.

He crossed home plate and his teammates mobbed him, slapping him on the back, and congratulating him in obligatory fashion through their waves of prepubescent jealousy and undeveloped filial admiration. He removed his helmet and found his mother in the crowd. She was jumping and clapping, but her head seemed to be on some kind of desperate swivel, searching for something unidentified. It wasn't necessarily Peter Carrigan she was searching for; that's far too trite a conclusion to make about such a complex and undaunted woman; it was almost unbefitting to suggest it.

She was, however, the only person in the entire bleachers sitting alone. And John Carrigan began to cry with violent heaves of his chest, unable to catch his breath. He felt dizzy and bent over, his head in his lap. He wasn't sad, just compressed.

"Calm down, kid," said his coach. "That's just the adrenaline rush. There's a lot more where that came from. Come on Richie—you next; there's more space over that fence."

MAY 1, 2000

Summers had always been nondescript in John Carrigan's mind; a kind of ill-defined interim space between periods more accurately and distinctively marked by the products of time. This summer was to be a wall, a malaise that made each day indistinguishable from the others.

In the coming of the first ending, there were no scenes—just an anti-climax before a climax, and then eventually, a ticket home to a Dublin Carrigan hadn't seen since watching it go by from the back of a taxicab on the way to the airport after his father's funeral.

Jane Kiley sat anemically on the corner of Carrigan's bed on a Tuesday afternoon on the first day of May, but her eyes were heavy and pensive. And her chin was burdened with the weight of a seeming anger and annoyance; her hair fell into her face in a way that shrouded her mouth, but she made no attempt to move it. She tapped her left foot with frequent rushes of adrenaline, and sighed inconspicuously and raucously on several occasions—overtly begging Carrigan to question her, to serve her with a biting inquisition to alleviate the guilt of her message.

"It was out of my control," she would say. "He asked me to tell him. I had no choice."

"What's going on, kid?" Carrigan had finally spoken up, and his tone revealed a kind of insulted offense at being manipulated into it.

"John, I just need some time, John."

She hadn't used his first name in months and now she used it twice in the space of a single sentence. Carrigan surmised that the meaning was horrific—it seemed as if she wouldn't add to the blow by referring to him casually or affectionately or even sarcastically.

"What does that mean?"

"I just don't want to be consumed."

"But you still have the feeling?"

"What?"

"The inscrutable thing. The burrowing thing that finds the marrow of your bones. The thing you don't define."

"You're not even paying attention, John. This isn't about your ego—this isn't an abstraction."

"I'm sorry. I'm sorry. I'm listening. I understand."

"It has nothing to do with how I feel for you. I'm mad about you. And Christ, I don't think there'll ever be a time when I won't be." She cringed perceptibly, realizing immediately that she shouldn't have said that, shouldn't have promised a feeling—that seemed to be the issue at hand. "I'm coming back John. This is not the end of us."

She hid her cringe here, but the violation was even deeper, so deep that maybe it was hidden from her as well; no one leaves, at least in the way that Jane was leaving, if she is genuinely planning on returning. The desire to return overwhelms the uncertainty broached by the physical act of the leaving.

She continued on her speech, "But my affection, my desire, my awe of you is my identity and it kills me. I get in these little trances and actually forget to breathe sometimes just contemplating all of it. And I'm ashamed. I really am embarrassed at myself; I'm not some gushing, writing-your-name-in-my-notebook kind of sweetheart, you know. I'm no good for you like this. I'm no good for you when I relinquish myself for you—"

Carrigan's reaction was violent and loud. His pitcher's right arm whipped his keys recklessly and with full force at the wall, and cut a jagged black line into the withering white paint.

"I never asked that of you! Ever! It's always been you that I've wanted—you in the action and spirit of who you are. You as defiant and free and sly and mischievous. I never wanted some fan, some admirer who affirms me. Some sycophant who reveres even my destructions."

"Stop."

The simple and unelaborated-upon admonishment was all he deserved for such too conscious tripe.

"So you can massacre me and I don't get to respond?"

"It's a contest now?" Jane's anxiety was quickly being replaced by frustration, and she found her empathy waning.

"No—I'm just saying; it's only fair that—"

"Just don't make speeches, J." (She was oddly growing more affectionate as her footing grew stronger and her empathy fully fell away, but still could not bring herself to call him Carrigan; it seemed like it would be poor form and an improper belittling of a dying opponent, like a consciously misleading symbol suggesting that she might change her mind when her resoluteness was startling.)

"And you may not have wanted those things from me—you may not even like them, but you do crave them, J. You've come to need them from me. You adore the worship even if you hate that you adore it. It's borderline cherishing and you just crumble when I don't give it to you. You become fragile and wanting and I created that in you. But I don't think you realize that you act that way. I do think you'd quit if you did. I do believe that you'd run from who you are in those moments. And can't you let yourself be inarticulate for one damn moment—to just curse or fumble or spit?"

Jane started to curse wildly, and incoherently, and now with almost no sentence structure, but just a coarse and emphatic repetition of all of the vulgar slurs she had ever come across, loudly hitting the consonants with a vigor that spewed saliva from her mouth. It was the most raw and sexual thing Carrigan had ever witnessed and he physically yearned for her with a sorrow signifying a belief that she had surpassed him, and that he could never have her now, realizing it just now, at the very moment that his desire had reached animalistic proportion.

"Oh don't look so appalled, John. I'm ruining the memory for you? I know you think it. Because I'm not fawning or sorry or pausing to remember, or giving you a mental photograph that you could still frame and tell to the next one of me for sympathy or darkness or feigned mystery."

Carrigan ran his left hand gruffly over his unshaven face in an attitude of pure rage, that only served to disguise his desire. He was virtually breathing from his eyes—every other orifice was locked in righteous and petulant and furious disbelief. His body craved her. His ego crumbled at her feet—she had surpassed him, or had always been surpassing. He could not have her like this—she would not have him with him like this, and her with the footing that she was finding anew with each vulgarity-laden epitaph.

"Stop. It's not really your fault, John. I leave now because I want it to end up as me and you. I'm sure of that, by the way."

It wasn't actually a lie; she suddenly believed in it as she said it (a belief generated by her ability to read the raw desire in his breath; a trait she had been begging for since the first night she relented to him) and that's all one can ask for when it comes to honesty, and there was no affect in her voice, or the shakiness or treble that accompanies a guilt-infested lie.

"I don't want some vivid disaster that becomes another notch on emotional timelines. I want you. I love you. I only don't want to be someone that you'll grow to despise, or worse, grow to be bored with."

She kissed him softly and knowingly on the mouth. She was completely certain in her leaving. This was her only sadness about the entirety of the affair—that she had no doubt; that once she began, she made no pause. She smiled warmly, and with her eyes closed, signifying a proper measure of melancholy—signifying significance in the action of leaving. It wasn't for his memory. She felt it again.

"I'll give you whatever you want," said Carrigan, his voice becoming demure and steadied, his faith strangely and almost obscenely starting to be restored in the inscrutable thing. A quick and seductive sense of liberation washed him—he had seemed to keep the feeling of the whole thing while simultaneously emancipating him from the real and daily requirement to oblige and ratify it with poignancy or eventfulness. It could live on its own now, and could not be killed because it lived in a place separate from life, separate from the aching physical inadequacy that accompanies the day to day living of it in the shadow of another living, worthy thing.

He breathed deeply, and remembered a request his friend Alex had made for him to come to Foxwoods Casino and play in a high stakes game of Texas Hold-em that night; the local games didn't run on Tuesdays and he had denied Alex's request with the anticipation of meeting Jane for a late-night slice of pizza or a tempestuous walk under a shallow moon. Both were chores he no longer had to fulfill.

He loved the game because he found money was an obscene oddity of human invention; poker was still a game to him, still just a pure opportunity to think more deeply than a stranger sitting across a green-felted table from him, still just a chance to climb inside that man's entire psyche just by using only natural instinct and memory and verve. An hour drive up I-95 and he could be in that place apart, and play until dawn or until whenever he finally felt the unquenchable need to eat or sleep or stop himself from getting sick. In this moment he became vital, almost excited that she could go now but that he would not lose her. Or more accurately, that he could avoid losing her by the bravery-laden act of going.

He walked her through the gates of his building and out onto Temple Street with her. "I'm in love with you," he said softly, kissing her on the forehead and caressing the smooth skin on the small of her back under her faded grey t-shirt. She leaned into him, holding his neck with her left hand. He suddenly needed her, like never before, to come back in and mingle that smooth skin with his and with the worn sheets of his too-small bed. He mustered his final ounce of resolve, or dignity, or abstract stupidity, and kept the craving to himself.

"Goodbye, Carrigan."

Carrigan made it over the Q bridge and outside of New Haven will full breath in his lungs and strength still deep in his stomach, his borrowed car riding smoothly, stridently, and travelling in a straight, unwavering line. He was excited for the game, and liberated by a singular feeling of being alone and not panicking, by having her still but not needing her shadow or affect or reprobation. But the radio didn't go on, and he hadn't noticed that he was travelling in a kind of maniacally focused silence. He was perceivably entranced, determined—in a tenuous struggle to maintain a mindset that had been only just now conjured.

Exit 53. Carrigan's stomach wavered, in a brief but startling fit of nausea and doubt.

"East Haven is a putrid stench-burgh," he muttered aloud and laughed briefly, the laughter disrupting the fragile serenity in the clutches of his stomach. The car kept driving on.

Exit 60. Carrigan's breathing shallowed sharply and without warning, and he was confronted with that violent kind of one-time, percussive hiccup that assaults the chest and throat, made all the more painful by the complete lack of preparation there is for its coming. Carrigan writhed in pain but believed it to be a physiological event. The car kept driving on.

Exit 63. Halfway. He stopped for gas at the rest area. He peered over at the McDonald's that he had never failed to enter on his way to a game. He wasn't hungry. But realizing that in the day's eventfulness he had not eaten anything, he walked towards the door, but without purpose and with a persistent desire to look back over his shoulder, to look backwards towards the direction of home. There were five people ahead of him in line as he unnecessarily studied a menu that he had committed to memory, the remnants of a thousand post- or pre-game fast food indulgences ever-present on his sensory tongue.

After five minutes, there was only one person left ahead of him. This was it—do or die. Eat and drive forward, or abandon the escape and head backwards. *Gatsby's* final line was penetrating his skull with a kind of physical force—"So we beat on, boats against the current, borne back ceaselessly into the past." He was ashamed at such a ubiquitous reference in a time that seemed to deserve so much more nuance and scarcity and insular obscurity—he couldn't even conjure any Eliot or Auden?

The crucible decision was made for him. The girl behind the counter had barely opened her mouth, and hadn't finished the line, "How can I help you?" when a force bigger than himself or his will drove Carrigan quickly into the restroom. He vomited immediately and without any possibility of deciding whether he wanted to or not. This seemed like a brutal and mocking intrusion on his liberty, and he lamented his state with a loud and sorrowful groan, easily audible to anyone else in the cavernous public restroom between exits 62 and 63 of the northbound corridor of I-95. And he was terrified to find that even in the immediate instant following his sudden sickness, he did not feel better; he did not find relief. This terrified him, and virtually blinded his apoplectic eyes with tears of rage and sorrow and futility, and again, just as an hour or so earlier, craven sexual desire.

He walked directly back to his car and drove in the direction of New Haven with a fierce rapidity—an eagerness of purpose if not with a design or a confidence in a discernible outcome, maintaining a wild belief that if he could remain in the vicinity of the sorrow, of the vanquishing, than he could understand it, and manipulate it—bend it to his will like he was sure men of words and passion and charm and depth did—that he could stem the rising tide of Fitzgerald's caustic and bitter closing line (perfect despite its ubiquity, or maybe that's just how they become ubiquitous); if he remained where the carnage occurred, then his movement would not be an unnatural migration backwards, would not be a recycling of some false and over-glorified past, but instead a vigilant allegiance to an authentic feeling, whether that feeling yielded requital or brutality or death, or at least a kind of death. There must be a reward for that. John Carrigan was sure of it. All of this paced through his mind in virtual essay form as he travelled. The car drove frantically, weaving from lane to lane this time, in the direction of home. New Haven.

Jane Kiley had been suddenly reanimated as a woman who didn't want him, as a woman who didn't care if she had him; as a woman who was clearly beyond him, at least now, if not always. And in her disavowal she was instantly and pathologically reborn in verve and insight and independence and style for Carrigan—in distrust and despair and desire and urgency and in that aching, grating, all-absorbing sickness that too often each day escaped the heart and radiated to the vulnerable and undefended stomach that only served to acknowledge his frailty and inconsequence and lack of kingship, nobility, and grace.

He woke the next morning to the commencement of the period of time in which he could not sleep. His instinctual dreams of her (sexual, intellectual, cinematic, mean-spirited; the whole tableau) startled him awake—he feared them; he could not allow them to exist if he was not sure he could make them the truth. And the decree of absence had shaken that understanding; it was incessantly and cruelly worse than bad moments that he could make sense of. He was afflicted with the persistent terror that all of this meant nothing to her, that she had already become unrecognizable to the truth of his memory and his addiction to his faith in her affection. And he knew that if he asked her, he would instantly mean nothing to her.

And so he existed under a crippling catch-22, for any actual and overt attempt to extinguish these phantoms of doubt would ensure either their initiation or guarantee their permanence, as they would reveal him to be a man too weak and too ineffectual to wait for her natural return, and revealing him to be the kind of scared, covetous, infantile and insecure beggar that everyone else never even seemed to bother to try hiding, and that she had accused him of in her own consciousness for some time now.

He was involuntarily waking by 4:00 am on most days. He took to taking exceedingly long walks to destinations he didn't care to go to. The journeys could maybe, he hoped, serve to revive his paralyzed ambition, could release the tsunami of frantic energy that now permanently consumed his stomach. More importantly, they could waste hours in the day, and contribute to the singular effort of vanquishing days from this infernal and nondescript calendar of doubt and misery, waiting for her decision, he supposed. He always imagined her speaking from a great pulpit—like Father Mapple (he only had ubiquitous references now) in his fiery admonitions against hubris and violations of nature. Who did she think she was? Carrigan wondered this aloud often on his walks (though the question was rhetorical and unbefitting, as she had become someone he coveted with an intensity he could not recognize), and nodded his head sardonically and theatrically, all the while though having no room in his soul to harbor any animosity. He was completely consumed by the result of her impending judgment. He could muster no other feelings or speculations. He couldn't even sit still to watch a ballgame or a movie or sit in a poker game for more than 30 minutes (he had played for 16 hours the day before she left).

Most of all, he sought sleep, but while the walks proved successful in depleting his body, they were unsuccessful in helping him sleep. He would return by 6:00 am and lie awake with the throbbing, burning pain and weight of exhaustion in his eyes, or escape into sleep briefly only to be startled awake by thoughts of an instant that recalled to him his waking grief, which was seeming insurmountable by the advent of the second week (had it only been eight days?), and he had no handle on it. He was consumed. His body had been colonized and then tyrannized by an inconsolable brand of dependency, a feeling wholly new to him, a feeling with at least equal consequence to any single moment he had spent cooling in the embrace of her shadow. By the advent of June, it was only too clear to Carrigan that she had avoided the "consumption" she was so passionately guarding herself against that Tuesday afternoon at the outset of May, and misery had been vengefully joined by bitterness and whatever the thing is that arrives after fear is proven righteous, in the well of Carrigan's perpetually empty stomach.

JUNE 4, 2000

The bitterness alone did forge a rally of desperate pride in Carrigan by the 4th of June—he made an attempt to leave without vanishing, an attempt to find something in New Haven, or even New England that he could be about other than his diminished romantic capacity. He took the Amtrak train to Boston's South Station and walked patiently over to Fenway Park—Red Sox baseball was his only real connection to his father's American life.

He could distinctly remember sitting by his father 20 rows behind the first base dugout on both of their first journeys to Fenway. He wondered now where his father got the money for such tickets.

It would also be his father's last trip to Fenway. He remembered his father insisting to his mother that they come alone. It was June of 1985. Carrigan was six years old. Roger Clemens took a perfect game with 14 strikeouts into the 9th inning. He retired the first two batters like they were the cardboard cutouts of players that John had posed for pictures next to in the atrium, and the crowd rose to its collective feet. Cal Ripken Jr. stepped in for the Baltimore Orioles.

First pitch—sinking fastball that caught the back of the outside corner. Unhittable. Cal was wise to take it. Called strike one.

Second pitch—hard-splitter. Ripken just waived at it, seeing something that wasn't there. Strike two. The crowd grew frenzied. Begging almost for the completion of perfection in a city that had had none since the selling of Babe Ruth for a Broadway pipe dream, or perhaps long before that.

Third pitch—slider. Hung in the middle of the zone. Ripken battered the green monster for a two out double. No perfect game. No no-hitter. No explanation of why Clemens would throw his third best pitch in at the most crucial moment of, if not *his* life, surely at least ten thousand of the thirty-six thousand people in the ballpark that day. The crowd was devastated. This was the Red Sox—strokes of brilliance and romantic failure; it took a melancholy valor to having passion in them. And the failure never came with any explanation or rationale or solace. It was brutal; Carrigan instantly recalled the butchering of a lamb that he had accidentally witnessed through a creaked-upon door at the neighborhood market.

Clemens retired the next hitter quickly and indiscreetly and the Sox won 5-0. The crowd perked up some. Carrigan's father removed his son's dirty grey Sox cap that was two sizes too big and tousled his son's hair. But he was visibly disappointed. It was a sadness behind the eyes that even a willful father couldn't keep from his son with all his effort. And he wasn't even trying very hard; he was overcome. Carrigan never could erase that sorrow from the memory of his father's eyes; it was, in truth, his only completely discernible memory of him. But why did it bother him so deeply? The failure was Clemens', was it not?

And on this day, when the crowd jovially chanted along to Neil Diamond's "Sweet Caroline" during the 8th inning, Carrigan found himself to be the only person in the cathedral that is Fenway unable to lose himself in the frivolity and melancholic joy of the whole atmosphere. He would have to go. He would have to flee. Another scorched temple, and no more bricks to hurl, and no energy to hurl them or hope of accuracy if he gained any. He left without eating a hotdog.

JULY 14, 2000

Carrigan registered for Trinity College Dublin's final summer session on the last day of open registration. He was assigned a room in Botany Bay, the shrouded and ancient haunt of Professor Liam Keating. The only elective remaining was "Life-Writing, the study and practice of memoir, diary, journal, and the epistolary novel."

Carrigan tackled his first open submission in two tiers—one for public consumption and one for private analysis, though they were both acts of personal flagellation, akin, at least somewhat he thought, to the zealots who whipped themselves mercilessly to mimic Christ's passion in the hope of driving the plague from Europe in the 14th century.

He presented his project as a "true" letter that he had already sent back home, but he parenthetically annotated his own copy in mocking judgment of his own sentiments and the perceived willingness of his colleagues to believe any tripe that he spat out. Neither element was true or representative—he had become entirely detached, as he imagined the brain stem was detached from the spine during cataclysmic injury that caused paralysis or the death of the mind. What it really was was a send-up, or unflinching portrait, of the man he gravely feared he had become by the time Jane had left. This man sickened him. He thought that was at least a good start—his ability for revulsion—but he was not hopeful it would yield anything so it had no real embalming quality.

Dear Jane,

I'm supposed to journal for Trinity and present an abstraction of it to the group, and the only premise is that it be something from my observation that people might find interesting. And while there is a pervasive kind of arrogance (classic trick to fool dumb people and win arguments—acknowledge yourself as something unseemly and then appear humble by taking responsibility for it, and arrogance was the best one; the irony was just seductive) *ingrained in reading something entirely about myself for such an exercise, I think that, essentially, people are what people find interesting. And though broken, I guess I'm finally a person* (a part of the huddled mass; being a "person" was all rot; anybody and everybody was already doing it. Maybe I had become a person, but it was against my better wishes). *And though broken, being a person is just so much better than being an idea* (a pretty line that vacationing summer undergraduates would find riddled with depth). *And I was a 21-year-old with athletic and intellectual glory, a 21-year-old who had averaged 23.4 points a game during his sophomore season, had a play accepted for publication by the Rep, and had been to the National Spelling Bee and Little League World Series as a kid, for Christ's sake, and I hated that I could even potentially be about anything other than metaphysics and contemplation* (this one was vanity's masterstroke –aggrandize yourself in the forum of an artistic class assignment so you can let your classmates know just how epic you are without coming off as a braggart, and the part about the play wasn't even the truth. Double shot). *And just look at all this vainglorious and embarrassing self-confession I'm already induced into* (true, but it was self-induction).

My life had been this kaleidoscopic convergence of happenings, all of which demanded my own solitude, demanded the abject maintenance of my Keatsian anticipatory fervor (yes, that was it—throw in a bit about Keats and the Literature 101 geniuses think you're a real writer), *demanded that my imagination be untouched by, well, my life. But I didn't just dream of you; I lived inside of you and next to you and I didn't leave after it got beautiful—I couldn't because every time I tried it just kept getting more beautiful as it got more real, and how persistently cruel is it that something like that can actually happen?* (This was all true. I annotate here because it may be the only line where every syllable is true. Well, at least in an ephemeral way, particularly the part about it turning cruel).

And I thought my life was about so many things, but you see, it turns out that when you're in love, your life is entirely and sublimely and masochistically about that; it saturates the senses, really, and it is the lens through which all observation filters (okay, so this was somewhat true as well, but only when it went bad). *And I'm in love with you. But you know that. And you knew it before I ever wrote it down. So I suppose there is no arrogance in this because there is no choice in it* (a nod to the Gods; it makes you seem timeless—like history can judge you but temporal beings can't understand—you've reached a higher plane here).

And so I write now directly to you, as every word I've ever written has really been to you or for you or about you, or at least the hope of you (dreadful and blatant perjury). *It is that feeling that makes me a writer, or at least makes me care about being one* (I was not a writer; I would never allow myself the title if I was the other listener). *And I announce to you before I even start that what this really is is an exercise in redundancy, for every line will transfigure into one line –I miss you* (i.e.—I need you in a way I loathe).

I didn't know it until I knew it, I guess—but I guess you can't write your way into things or charm your way out of them. I was wrong to wrap my arms around you when you needed to go away. I wasn't wrong on purpose and I was wrong for all the right reasons, but I was still wrong (nope—absolutely righteous and I'll take that to the grave. False apology—wasn't that a sign that you had the evil in you?). *I didn't know any better; I was scared for the first time in my life, and the purity of that fear and the depth of the sadness evoked by what was going away separated me from myself* (This one is still pending. I merely hope it separated me from myself, but I was a disaster this summer. Yes, I can't even poeticize it; disaster is as good as it gets here). *I was too scared to rely on nature, which is what makes us worthwhile anyway. We didn't create this; it made us* (A natural reaffirmation. Perhaps redundant, but nature comes in cycles—the wittier ones will get this use of imagery).

Because the thing is, I let myself try and see someone else (more perjury). *And the thing is, it's actually been, well, good. And the thing is, the fact that it is good makes all the difference for what I'm writing to you, for if it was bad the truth would still be shrouded in circum-*

stance—instead, it reveals. You see she's gorgeous and she's smart; she's passionate and provocative, interesting and eclectic. She is so many things, but the one thing she is indomitably and irrevocably not makes all the difference—she is not you (personalize it and bring it home here). *Time doesn't change that, and there is nothing in me, nothing even hidden in despair, that will ever wish that it could. You're the one I think of. You're the one I want to walk through the day with, and you're the one I want to talk to about all of the things we can't walk through together* (but you wanted them separate Jane, and in truth, so did I. Yours is the only face I see when I close my eyes. (I saw nothing when I closed my eyes now)).

The truth of that is one I'll never escape; it's like a golden prison and I am in love with it (Ahh! I cringe at even the sight of this horrid line—nothing but sentiment, wretched, cynical writing). *The big stuff was hard and we weren't ready for it, but the moments were just so good, and on that last day when everything in the world told you to say no, you looked through me and simply said, "I'm so in love with you." And there's a truth in that, too. We looked from the wrong direction; we never had to "figure anything out," and we don't have to now. We can just be, and being is the power and the glory all by itself* (I bet these pukes don't know too much Graham Greene; I'll probably get away with swiping his verbiage, and even the ones who notice might consider it well-timed homage).

We ran to each other at 3 in the morning because we had to find each other, and it didn't matter if we had seen each other the hour before or would see each other again when the sun came up (that happened once. I think she lost her keys). *And that's the kind of passion that never gets forfeited, that never gets substituted for. And so I'm not going to seek you and I'm not going to persuade you, but instead ask you only this—that when that moment comes when you miss me in a way that you don't want to fight, just promise you'll tell me—no matter what the circumstance is for either of us* (an achingly fair request). *And if you promise to do that, I'll promise to let it be all the days in between* (the final installment of the perjury chronicles). *I'm going to win you back, love, but not by trying, just by living. And so now I get to write the best line I've ever written—I love you, Jane Kiley* (that was perfect; end by including her name.

They all picture her now and the hurt becomes real).

JWC

Had he really been so worthless, and so pious, and worst of all, unfunny? The lack of humor stood out to him as the most grievous offense. It was August 15th as he looked over his annotated draft, bored and rather mortified (intellectually at least; his emotional detachment remained) by the eager acceptance of his classmates for the non-annotated version of his epistle, and slightly appalled at himself for the macabre ease in which he could write things that he did not mean, or for the purpose of the flagellant. He had always done it, and had always justified it in the sense that if the purpose mattered, then the sentiments need not be true. This was the first time he had dissected it in a scholarly fashion, however, (perhaps motivated to re-examination by the abject futility of this romantic ordeal) and he was frightened at just how elusive he could be, or more accurately, how willing almost all of his peers were to digest and even covet his ability for stage sentiment. But in the ability to mock-up his own degradation, a strange power did absorb him, but it was budding at best; he saw no Jane in it.

Dublin was lost to him for now. As with the alacrity and confusion of his father's funeral, his wall of malaise made the city an impersonal blur to him still. The River Liffey's evening colors were only objectively picturesque inside this wall, not passionate or vivid or lurid. And it was this way, too, with the serenity of St. Stephen's Green being only understood by proxy of observance, and the energy of Grafton Street only reported to him by the experience of others. He took one last haunting look into each of the rooms on Botany Bay's second floor, each of the places that Professor Liam Keating could have lived and pontificated and written, could have fled from drenched in the intrusive blood of Ulster and away from the only woman his young heart had pledged to love; but Carrigan's connection to history remained wanting as of now.

On August 25th of the millennium New Year, Jane Kiley was waiting on Carrigan's doorstep as he sauntered through the same gates they had parted ways at some months before.

"I told you I was coming back." She was smiling sheepishly, expectant of a kind of reunifying embrace that was never in doubt—the summer was a block of nondescript interims of more eventful times, after all.

Carrigan was struck—he hadn't done anything. He had just left. Perhaps more leaving could only do him better.

"I can't right now," he said. "Just not right now, not right at this minute."

He walked into a hidden area of the courtyard and breathed deeply, feeling no nausea, for a fleeting, confused moment at least. The power and the glory. He cried profusely, unsure of exactly why, but deeply suspecting the worst elements in him had not been fully expunged by his exodus and Jane's return.

OCTOBER 31, 2000

It was the end of an insipid Indian summer. Yesterday was a day of bare, lithe, collegiate skin protruding from soft-colored dresses of relaxed patterns and lazy stitching. It was a day of deep must and too-easily acquired perspiration, and a day of lazy sexual innuendo and the promise of endless and vapid tomorrows, where both apathy and antipathy could be excused by the promise of the next vapid tomorrow. And when the Indian summer appeared to be ready to extend its seemingly benign austerity all the way into November, Carrigan concluded that he needed to find a new term to categorize it, for this was a new kind of temperate dominance—a kind of temperate homogeny that surely no New Englander had ever been forced to bear before. Yes, he was the first, and this was his cross; a solemn, if imagined cross, made all the more maddening because absolutely no one cared. And Carrigan surely hated summer—a season where all one could feel was his own comfort, or his own exhaustion. A season of nothingness, for one cannot argue that comfort is a something, or at least anything more than the absence of a tangible pain.

But today the leaves were red, and red without warning or the luxury of anticipation. They were a burnt red, and they crackled rigidly under Carrigan's soft, brown, laced-up boat shoes, shoes he wore for all seasons, and shoes that had never actually seen the deck of a boat (a negligent Irishman), as he walked towards class. This was the first true day of his last year of philosophy; the intrusively low-hanging sun and its accompanying malaise had robbed him of the first two months of his senior campaign. But Carrigan was used to this sort of robbery, used to a kind of life where beauty came without warning, and everything departed without an epilogue. It was a life where pathos was wasted on those who already had it. His last year had arrived today and tomorrow it would be November. He swiftly decided that Eliot was wrong; April had no monopoly on cruelty, and then he even more quickly decided to be embarrassed at the kind of affectation that would allow him to even privately consider such a wretchedly mundane and sophomoric thought (Eliot had returned to him only in widely known epigrammatic form). Leave the sophistry to the self-congratulatory sophomores, he thought, and then he couldn't decide if all epigram was sophistry, and before he had finished this rumination, his first class had ended, and the morning had become noon.

The bitterness of the new autumn wind was unsettling, and Carrigan, to his own abject surprise, ducked inside a familiar academic office building on Trumbull Street to seek a momentary reprieve. Carrigan believed that he defied the fecklessness of seasons that fell too quickly away by reading non-germane text, and slowing down when the day sped up, but this was a kind of affectation too. His favorite pastime was to sit pensively and alone in the audience of Woolsey Hall, during a time in which he had class, while the symphony practiced, or that is, warmed up to practice, and Carrigan could hear that cacophony of sound produced when individual instruments are played in disregard to the rhythm, focus, and timing of the brass and woodwind brethren they shared the stage with. He fancied that he could hear each individual player at work at his own, solitary craft amidst all the chaos and competition. It was a nice thought.

Once inside the ancient (for America) edifice, he knew his destination, and he ascended a back, dilapidated staircase where the fourth and eighth steps were in need of repair, and where the complete denial of any attempt to make these repairs was equal parts quaintness and arrogance of a place that people might complain about but would surely never abandon. He was never sure whether he wanted that door at the end of the second floor's initial corridor to be open or not, and he tortured himself in pondering this fact as he walked slowly towards it. To not walk in to that specific door when open would be to commit a kind of lechery against himself; to signify that he was moving on to something more efficient than the conversations he found within. To signify a distaste for something he could never bear being distasteful of. It was Prof. Keating's door, and he loved him deeply and without qualification, like a father whom you never have to see lose brilliance or fall down, or be challenged, or grow old or be lied to about. As a freshman, he had been a Monsignor Darcy to Carrigan, and never once fell short of even the literary ideal. Now he supposed that they were friends, and Keating had even declared it to be so, but Carrigan had never wanted it to be so. For him, theirs was a different kind of love, and friendship is the death of reverence. He couldn't lose any more revered things—he had no more bricks to throw at the temple, remember; they all belonged to Jane now.

Keating's white hair was sloppy, but supple, and his lean, tall figure carried no more than 145 pounds. He was now 76, but his poor hearing was no testament to his age—he had ruptured an eardrum when the British brought the full throat of their remaining colonial desire to crush humble little Donegal, on the borderland between the republic and the past in '44, and some of the IRA chaps ended up standing too close to grenades, or just close enough to their consciences. Of course, Keating and Carrigan shared this bit of reverie too, but it was not a thing that needed to be discussed, or really could be without an interrogation of the Irish past that both men (was Carrigan a man?) were unwilling and unready (even at 76 in Keating's case) to consider.

They instead talked of Whitman for hours, and reread books from the angles of minor characters, and embellished romantic moments and believed in the future. Keating refilled his whiskey glass liberally; a testament to their intimacy, or a testament to something he couldn't control, and Carrigan never dared to even consider which it was. He had nine children, and could think about them abstractly and poetically without ever losing the intimacy and irrationality of a father. He was a man who had drawn blood and hated violence. He was a man who loved his wife and mourned her passing not as the loss of a companion, which could be replaced, but as the loss of a feeling, which of course couldn't even be remembered. His heart was deep and it was only broken when it deserved to be. Carrigan loved him. And he had told him eloquently and without pretense about Jane the last time they had talked.

All Keating would say in response was, "I like her very much."

It seemed like a kind of cruelty, and it was, actually, but not all cruelty is cruel.

The door at the end of the initial corridor on the second floor was closed. Carrigan closed his eyes, and exhaled into a deep relief with his back resting plaintively on the dreary, grey wall, before hurrying out of the corridor; another day safe for reverence.

He made it to Woolsey Hall too late—the symphony had come together now, and they played with an easy beauty that was remembered.

And he wasn't alone in the audience—Jane Kiley sat six rows up and to his left. They hadn't spoken since the outset of August, and Carrigan had spilled no ink. He automatically moved to her, and affixed the look of exiled romance into his gaze. She stood up before he could measure her, and she left. No one could say she left dramatically or cinematically. In fact, in her countenance, she brought to mind the "pallid hue" of Faulkner's dead Emily. And even then Carrigan saw that she didn't leave because she was angry. She didn't love him. She didn't love him right now, is a more accurate way to articulate it. And he instantly mourned it like the loss of a feeling, so much so that he failed to even deride his own wickedness. Now she was just vacuous and depleting remembrance; her taste was gone. He forgot to exhale for several moments. He stirred with a violent fit of coughing, so obstreperous that many of the practicing musicians paused to scowl at him.

That 5:30 deep October dusk found him in Basset Park, the lone shooter on an auburn leaf-ridden basketball court. It was oppressively auburn—no yellow, no orange, and not a hint of anything that remained green. He shot obsessively, and it was not for practice; this was a craft he needed no practice at. The thickening mist, which was seemingly becoming sleet, blackened his hands as the wet ball careened off the damp blacktop. He felt more at ease the more the gloom gathered, as the promise of his own solitude in a place he had returned to since his father placed a ball in his hands seemed more secure. His father was dead now and he remembered that death here and only here. His mother remained either too devastated or not devastated enough; he couldn't understand which, but then again he didn't try to decode her sentiment very arduously. The reverberation of the twine as the ball ripped softly or domineeringly through it had always been his favorite sound, a repeatable sound that came with accomplishment, and more importantly, divinity. No one had ever told him how to shoot—it would've been redundant; there was never a moment when he wasn't great, at this at least. That reverberating, approbating swoosh of twine was still his favorite sound long after people stopped cheering for it.

He kept shooting, unconsciously almost, and the gathering gloom (it's a hackneyed phrase but when gloom gathers, it must be recognized as such) became suddenly infiltrated by artificial light and deafening noise. He turned and looked into the neighboring streets—little zombies and witches and goblins and vampires with plastic pumpkin buckets scoured the streets for lit houses, as their parents trailed them and beckoned with voices of over-affection or disquiet.

"Put that jacket back on, Parker!"

"Don't eat anything yet!"

Carrigan, affronted by the dilemma of a suburbia that just doesn't seem infused with enough tragedy (or at least Irish tragedy) or pathos to make happiness seem like success, dribbled out of the park and gave his wet basketball to a nine-year-old President Clinton. He didn't see any artifice in the maze of masks.

The next morning opened to a four-inch covering of rich, white snow. That first snow that has no brown mitigation; untouched by human hands or the concern for human alacrity. There was no more auburn. From Indian summer to resonant winter. The phone rang at 9:29 am. Professor Liam Keating had died reading in his office sometime the previous afternoon. Was he alive when Carrigan hesitated on the stairs and dead by the time he arrived at the door? Carrigan made the sign of the cross and sunk into a deep, dreamless sleep. Autumn had lasted one day this year.

NOVEMBER 2, 2000

By the middle of the day after Prof. Keating's death, Carrigan's sleep was no longer dreamless. In fact, he dreamt with intent and purpose; his dreams were a preamble to an event he would get to live very shortly. He dreamt of Jane Kiley. There would be a funeral. There would be an opportunity, and maybe the only pure one he could ever get with her again.

In short form, Carrigan had loved Jane Kiley at approximately four distinctly different times. He loved her longingly the first day he met her, when they were both freshman and she had a boyfriend, and he knocked on her door to take her roommate to an awful movie at the old York Square theatre. As he sat through that film, he knew even then that he didn't love her simply because she was the other—the girl who was not the disappointment sitting next to him who couldn't name any of *The Beatles* and who was too aggressively slotting her arm into his. No, Jane was exactly Jane—the utter lack of self-consciousness, the complete absence of affect, the dark, true sarcasm in her jokes that nevertheless didn't infringe on the cynical, and those aquatic eyes. She was the intensity of the urbane and the random; the beauty and potentiality of the nondescript meeting. He loved her hopefully and wildly that first day, and that awful movie was bearable because its end would bring him back to her door. It was a day when none of his sentiments were saccharine because he actually meant them. He was even glad the roommate was so wretched, for he would feel less in need of penitence when he pretended to like her for a few more weeks to have an excuse to keep returning to Jane's door.

He loved her desperately during the time period in which she hated him for making her love him so crushingly while she was still with that boy that she couldn't leave because the boy was too sweet to have ever done anything mean to her. Carrigan tortured her during this period; this is a fact that could not be denied, but he believed he loved her with no affect, so his torture could, and maybe should, be forgiven. He tortured her with his awful benevolence. He would never ask for anything, or make any appeal for her guilt, which of course made her feel intensely guilty. He laughed disarmingly when she felt sorry for his sorrow. He pulled her into side rooms and made intense speeches and walked away before she could respond. He wrote her letters the day before he would be gone for weeks at a time. He knew what he was doing. He knew he was playing a role (in the time that he was exonerated for it because she wanted that as much as he wanted to play it), and he knew he was benignly dominating her covetous heart. He thought it was fair. The feeling was genuine, always. And maybe he thought he was doing her a favor—he had been close enough to feel that her feeling was genuine, too.

He loved her passionately for the first three months of the seven they spent together, officially at least (or, maybe, not so officially. Essentially is a more apt descriptor—both of them lived essentially much more than they ever lived officially). It wasn't about the past. And it wasn't about what could be coming. This was the time he could always distinctly and immediately remember, a time represented entirely by a single day, as anything worth doing could be. Love had to happen in a day, the need for compilation suggested for the need for aggregation, and that just wouldn't do. It was, in fairness, nothing in comparison to the love he felt for her now, but that did not render it unworthy or even lesser, but, in reality, exactly what it should be. Whitman taught Carrigan that in the preface to *Leaves of Grass*... "the corpse is slowly borne from the eating and sleeping rooms of the house…perceives that it waits a little while in the door…that it was fittest for its days…that its action has descended to the stalwart and well-shaped heir who approaches…and that he shall be fittest for his days." He wasn't supposed to love her the same way the whole time through. It was one thing about Jane that Carrrigan was content with.

DECEMBER 21, 1998

It was strange how the seasons worked, Carrigan thought. You progress all the way through a calendar only to find its shortest day with ten days to go. A kind of sardonic reminder that time would perpetually taunt man—the year a kind of cavernous maze you made it through only to find more impending darkness when you found the other end. There was not more time for this or for that, it seemed. There was now.

And in the quickly fading New Haven sunlight, even at just shy of 2:00pm, he sat across from Jane Kiley at an outdoor table in front of Sullivan's on Chapel Street. It was virtually balmy for December in New England; approaching 60 degrees and even the breeze wasn't altogether chilling. Jane wore a deep ocean blue dress that exposed a still tanned and smooth athletic left calf, under a black cardigan. Her soft brown hair was shiny and flipped wildly but fashionably into her face with the wind. Her blue earrings matched her aquatic eyes, which had mischief in them.

"You're different," she said.

Carrigan reflexively grunted and began to utter a defensive "come on!" when Jane grabbed his hand and soothed it gently.

"No, I mean better," she said. And she smiled and shook her head teasingly simultaneously.

"Wonderful to learn how treacherously awful I had been before," said a defiant Carrigan.

"Would you just shut up, you absurdly grandiose Irish pseudo-poet? I just mean, you actually look at me when you talk now."

"That's new," he said, and wondered if he was a pseudo-poet because he tended to dramatize ordinary things, or because he was a hack.

"Don't play dumb, Carrigan."

He loved that even after they were together, she stilled called him Carrigan. To call him John would be to signify some change in intimacy, some leveling or a timeline of feeling. No, he would always be Carrigan to her. A kind of monument to the endurance of that first instance of shared emotion.

"You used to look off into the distance or even over my head during every single word. Like you were performing a monologue to an imagined crowd and just hoped that I would be in some vast, ill-defined audience."

"That's pretty deep for a Thursday afternoon."

"Don't deflect, Carrigan. I'm trying to have a wonderful human moment with you, and say something nice. "

"Then be nice! That pseudo-poet remark really cut deep. A lesser talent might even recede into self-doubt from such mockery."

"This is never something I'd worry about."

"I'm serious. I might take up reading Dylan Thomas and walk alone in parks at night."

"You already do that."

"Yes, but never from sadness or self-doubt. Only because I'm just so much smarter and deeper and more well-read than you and your Judy Bloom obsession, and pro-capital New York Yankees admiration. Why are you smiling? I'm being terrible. At least somewhat ironically, but still terrible."

"But you looked at me the entire time, Carrigan. And I couldn't be nice without some form of temperance. You wouldn't believe me, or would worry that I was dying or something. Anyway, it's better. I adored you before. But I love you right now."

Carrigan blushed and said it back. He agreed with her and felt the same, but still, the words "better" and "now" cut deeply into him, finding the marrow. If they had traversed an imaginary landscape from adoration to love, then what was next? What would be the next change? Did there have to be one?

Carrigan didn't talk for quite a while. He ate his now cold cheeseburger lustily even though he was only mildly hungry. He needed a distraction. He felt guilty; he felt self-conscious. It was as if the letter in his pocket was the evidence of a kind of secret fraudulence that was still embedded somewhere inside of him. He felt that she must know; that she could see it in his face for sure. It was a stain he couldn't wash out.

Jane broke back in right on time.

"Okay, I have a completely non-leading or hinting type of question. It is a simple matter of artistic and subjective curiosity."

"You do realize that the phrase 'non-leading' is the epitome of what it means to lead, right? I mean, there really couldn't be a less leading proposal than the inclusion of a preface about leading. It literally leads the conversation in an almost physical direction."

"As I'm sure you realize that coyly and seemingly charmingly, but mostly obnoxiously, dissecting the syntax of someone's sentences is a ridiculously obvious way to subvert the reality of a situation."

"We're pretty big dorks, huh?" said Carrigan.

"Self-deprecation is another evasion technique," said Jane, "Though it is a bit more endearing. Particularly when you smile that smile that you think is roguish, but is really just adorably nerdy."

"Well, you're lucky you're beautiful, because you're just not as smart as you think you are. In fact, I was just thinking that you're quite fortunate that I'm a purely superficial knuckle-dragger who puts up with your pedantry only because you're so intoxicatingly gorgeous, and I can show you off to all of my friends."

"You have very few friends, and we never spend any time with them."

"Friendship is really more of a tacit bond than a physical interaction."

Jane fell silent, and paused with a wry smile on her face.

"Okay. Okay. You're right," said Carrigan. "I was just looking for an excuse to call you beautiful because I'm feeling happy, and if I had been only nice to you without some form of temperance you wouldn't believe me or would worry I was dying or something. Now, what was that question you were hinting at in your non-hinting way?"

"What?"

"I win," said Carrigan. "I successfully diverted you from the reality of the situation."

"Oh, oh. The question. Yes. What would you want your wedding song to be?"

"Well, Jane, call me old-fashioned, but I'd appreciate you getting down on one knee to make such an inquiry. I prefer all proposals made to me to be done in the form of supplication. It makes me feel all important, you know."

"I said your wedding song, not our wedding song, you smug Irish bastard."

(She added "Irish" to many of her pejoratives, playful or otherwise.

Carrigan often wondered who it was she was reminding about his heritage—the need to stress it so frequently).

"Well that's easy," said Carrigan. "'Angie', by the Rolling Stones."

"Well, what a fantastically superb answer that is, you nitwit. I mean it, that is virtually prize-winning in its stupidity."

"Go on," said Carrigan.

"It's got another girl's name in it, and it's about breaking up."

"So?"

"So?"

"Yeah, the song is purely phenomenal; Jagger even whispers during it. That trumps any petty concerns about semantics, names, or subjects. And I thought you were an artist. I have to say, I'm a little embarrassed for you."

They both laughed. Carrigan feigned getting on one knee, and Jane shoved him in the shoulder. He rose slowly and kissed her deeply, his path impeded at first by the shocks of hair that had fallen into her face. He pushed them back and caressed her lips softly with his own. He felt her tongue wrapped in his, and his heart beat faster. That made him smile; it wasn't their first kiss. He looked at her seriously for a few counts after they had finished kissing. Sarcasm was suspended for a time.

The hour bells of St. Mary's rang sonorously and Carrigan instinctively stood up.

"Old habits die hard," said Jane.

"What are you talking about?"

"You hear the hour bells and stand up like it's some kind of cue for you to depart, for the scene to be over. It's not a play, Carrigan. We are not bound by the opportune beauty of dramatic departures."

Carrigan started to speak in a predictably romantic tone; like a harsh and urgent whisper.

"Just stop," said Jane. "You know you're pretty damned entertaining and wonderful when you're not trying to prove how passionately in love with me you are."

"Shut up a second," said Carrigan. "I'm just trying to quote some Byron and get my profile shadow right in this light."

"I hate you," said Jane.

"I hate you back."

They laughed rhythmically together. They were happy. This was that third stage, the best stage, and Carrigan dreaded it for the abject impossibility of its permanence.

NOVEMBER 2, 2000

And he felt, as he woke at least, that he loved her deeply again today, in a reanimated way, in a way as deep as he had yearned for her with her hand on his neck and his hand unfurling her faded grey t-shirt on the day of her departure at the gates; the day of her ascension. And the day of Keating's funeral resembled some sort of panorama of the three other ways he had loved her, except for the fact that this time he loved her with a great sadness, and a great fear. A sadness only rendered because they had lost each other, and a fear only present because he wasn't sure he could regain it.

As Carrigan dressed for the funeral, he was reminded that, after all, he and Keating were not equals. Keating loved Carrigan with a kind of full bodied humanity; taking instant pride in his moments of greatness and spontaneous empathy and sorrow in his moments of sadness. He instructed Carrigan, but never for the existentiality of the lesson, but because he hoped that what he said might simply make the boy's life a little better, or a little fuller, and in the end, a little truer; a boy that he loved without description or comparison to other things that his heart enveloped. Keating was wonderful at love, a genius. And his life had been about only that. Only love for exactly what it was, and is.

Carrigan loved Keating (were they friends if they acted like friends, even if the bond was never equal?) because he worshipped him, and in truth, as with everything he loved up to this day, because of what it revealed to him about himself. But he didn't punish himself entirely for such a seemingly solipsistic outlook; it was merely a reminder of authenticity and divinity if a man like Keating could love him; it was something worth keeping. And he loved the qualities of Keating that he did not possess—that resolute and complete forfeiture of vanity and abject lack of human anxiety and want. And so it wasn't coldness or indifference to the death of the man that made him end his dreamless repose with requiems for Jane Kiley only. Instead, it was a love, and more importantly, a faith in the pure reach and wonder of him, which made him profoundly and uniquely unable to actually believe that Keating was dead, at least in any non-abstract construction. Or, conversely, or maybe even in addition to the realization that Keating was just the kind of man who would encourage John to see today, the day of his own respite, as an opportunity to find Jane once again.

Today's funeral was just another link on an invisible chain of human eventfulness that they held at opposing ends; one more thing that they shared without being in the same place. The funeral. An opportunity to stand next to Jane Kiley at a time when mundane grievance and the social propriety of yesterday were suspended, and in their places were pathos and a feeling of gravity which was quietly acknowledged to be more important than romantic disgust or the effects of even very bad behavior. Carrigan would have an opportunity to convince her to love him once again, and this time because he believed he missed her in a way that might not quit aching, or depart at all, even if she did. By 9:00 am, he was finally able to consider whether or not this would be the final link on that invisible chain he and Keating had held so stridently at opposing ends.

He dressed carefully, but not assiduously or formally. Grey pants. White shirt. Blue blazer. Navy blue tie slightly loosened. Brown boat shoes. Individual shocks of shiny brown hair pointing in independent directions, but not altogether uncombed. He made it to the foot of the great steps of St. Mary's by 10:30. Droves of similarly dressed young men with fervor in their eyes stood nonchalantly on Hillhouse Avenue. Some laughed languidly and carelessly, an awkward juxtaposition to the somber attitudes they would transform into as soon as it was time to mount the steps. Some of the more garish ones talked on cellular phones. The fervor in every set of eyes came from the same belief, a belief in a future of impact, a belief in a kind of assured greatness that remained in their eyes as even greater men before them continuously failed to find or seize it. It couldn't have been too long ago that a nearly 20-year-old, black-haired Liam Keating, dressed in grey pants and a blue blazer, stood outside a similar event, and held a similar fervor in his eyes. The fervor that only comes when one has no idea where he will go, and so can still believe that failure is for other people, and success is non-definitive. The years must have moved so quickly away for Keating, all muddled up and stolen from him by the obscene pace of joy and reverie and the practice of love. He had been pegged for that nondescript kind of greatness and verve. He wasn't like "other people." He wasn't bound to be "normal" or have his life measured only in good deeds and human kindness. He was pegged to be a man whose actions would be studied and debated. A man who would have statues built of him that some people would stand in protest in front of. But he did not publish. He did not rouse any man who didn't know him. He did not see Home Rule in his native land. And now he was 76 years old. And dead.

During his walk to the church, Carrigan had greedily pondered over a few questions. He worried over whom Keating's oldest daughter, Moira, would hug longest and most affectionately, knowing he would feel slighted if it wasn't him. He wondered if he should try to sit next to Jane, or just in her line of vision, and several less momentous concerns regarding blocking and scenery, and then felt a vague vulgar feeling of déjà vu for a departed element of his persona.

When he walked in, he immediately felt silly, and then that disappeared quickly due to the reason he felt silly; he only felt sad. It wasn't a link in a chain at all; it was the end of mortal flesh. Moira Keating had no role to play; she was just a woman bound to miss her father for the rest of her days. None of Prof. Keating's seven living children were dramatic figures, just lost adults who were clearly less prepared for the finality of it all than even Carrigan. Their mother Lauren's death hadn't struck them so deeply—their father had been there to assuage their melancholy with charm that was never poisonous or covetous or lustful. He was a great man.

Carrigan stood in the back of the church for the entirety of the ceremony, save the time he stepped backed into the great hallway, made the sign of the cross, and wept deeply and privately for seven continuous minutes.

As the recessional proceeded out of the back of the church, Jane gently grabbed Carrigan's arm and smiled a sorrowful grin as she walked by. He had not noticed her coming. Was her banal, soft, embracing gesture an acknowledgement of a love that remained, or the final gesture of feckless politeness for a life that had ended, and a moment that had died? Carrigan had no theories, not today. His friend was dead, and he was only sad. And he deserves acknowledgement, if only in a sketch, in these pages.

NOVEMBER 22, 1945

Liam Keating had come down into Dublin three and a half years earlier on the eve of his eighteenth birthday to take his degree (by special dispensation) at Trinity College. Now a senior, he lived in Goldsmith Hall, and found himself to be rather more remarkable than Oliver Goldsmith himself. He had just won the Beckett Prize for student drama, and was the best striker that anyone who knew Trinity football had ever seen. He was abusively handsome in his grey, upturned overcoat, with his wild black hair obscuring one of his steel blue eyes—abusively handsome because he belonged only to Megan Fitzpatrick, and no one could shake him from his oath, though many tried. She always missed him but never worried about him. He was a bold, chivalric and fascinating man who was never not fascinated by her. She lived in verse and spoke to Liam in silence. And they laughed together. Always, they laughed together. He was a giant, and this Ireland, in the current way it was constituted, could not be large enough for him as long as a foreign enemy held dominion over an acre of it.

So he suddenly took to speaking at Sinn Fein meetings (it was purely instinctual but not reckless) under the great arch near mid-campus, and on this day, Megan was with him, in a cobalt blue dress that was hidden by an ankle length black overcoat; her auburn hair protruding at its curly ends from under a grey knit cap. She was about ready to accuse him of timing his cadence to match the melody of the Dublin rain on the disfigured Trinity cobblestone, when the fury happened, and they would lose the abject pleasure of benign accusation.

With the war over in Europe months before, some of the younger and more spiteful British boys were looking for new ways to prove their nationalism, and had paired up with the Ulster Unionists to resume the pastime of disrupting Sinn Fein student assemblies. Today they lobbed rocks and cackled in cockney ignorance. What they hadn't planned for was the dozen or so Sinn Fein regulars and IRA cohorts who had come to hear Liam speak, and they drew pistols as soon as the first rock landed, but it was the Ulstermen who shot first. They killed James Bennett instantly, Liam Keating's roommate in Goldsmith who had only come down to the meeting because he had lost his own set of keys. And then the fury ensued, and Liam was quickly devoured and trampled by the crowd. He extricated himself, came to, and found Megan's overcoat slung languidly over the back of a bench, and Megan herself being beaten by the batons of two Ulstermen looking to deter such further insurrection—her cobalt blue dress smeared with rain and tears and blood and the devastating blackness of her running eye makeup. The Ulstermen had their backs to Liam as he approached, and were no match for his deft quickness and footballer's agility as he snatched the dagger from the back of the first man's belt, and instinctively stabbed them both piercingly and assertively; his final act of honor as the man who loved Megan Fitzpatrick without hesitation or melancholy. And as it turned out, it was the final truly active thing he would do in his time on earth, though he had no way of knowing that then.

It was the grace of his life that neither of them died; he was no artist with the dagger, and he sardonically (and in recollection, embarrassed by his too easy theatrics) recited "O, happy dagger" as he stood over Megan with tears shrouding his own wounded eyes, bathed in the blood of her assailants (he always cringed at the melodrama of the cliché when recalling the moment, and then felt guilty about caring about cliché in regards to such a moment). The next day he was on a four-hour train, and two-hour bus ride to Dingle in the west. The day after that he was on a two-week ship to America. The week after that, a three-hour train from Boston to New Haven. And then, following a delirious and semi-conscious courtship and the acceptance of a place hid away in academia, the love of, and marriage to, a woman who was not Megan Fitzpatrick.

NOVEMBER 10, 2000

John W. Carrigan
Prof. Mowbray
EN 373—Advanced Creative Fiction

With 12 hours to go until his original story was due, this was the extent of Carrigan's effort.

"It doesn't take much to be advanced," he wondered aloud. "Advanced." All one had to do was be one of the first 20 seniors to register for EN 373, and he gained the moniker "advanced." A hurdle-less race to the registrar for the title of burgeoning literary giant. And there were only 14 students in this section, so apparently there was no real competition at all—people could take it or leave it, like a free sandwich or a mildly entertaining conversation that passed the time slightly better than it whinnied the sensibilities. Carrigan thought that maybe they could bolster future registration if they attached more romantic adjectives to the title next semester—maybe "genius," or "visionary." But perhaps that wouldn't help either. Nobody really cared about those things now; they were quite arcane. Regardless, as the sonorous bells of St. Mary's rang their chimes of mocking ignominy until they signaled that it was 8:00 pm, Carrigan felt like a wretched fraud—a false talent at an endeavor that people didn't seem to care about anyway.

"I had a 60-line poem published in *The Review* last quarter," he had overheard Jack Lambert tell two absurdly and devastatingly attractive sophomores (devastating because they were so raucously unaware of the artistry in female beauty that profound) wearing short skirts and long sweaters and sporting willing and easy laughs, outside of Toad's last month.

"Oh, that's great. My brother actually just got an internship writing ad copy in New York," said the sophomore closest to Lambert.

"We won the co-ed intramural volleyball championship," was the reply from the second sophomore. She then lifted her cashmere sweater to show the navy blue t-shirt she wore underneath signifying the accomplishment, and showing a pierced navel and her tan (even in November), taught stomach.

It was only too clear to Lambert, and any random observers, that the three revelations of glory that were just made had a clear sense of co-equality to them. But Lambert was an agreeable sort, and happy to move along, and he quickly feigned impress and walked inside with his new friends. After all, they were outlandishly attractive, and it was only Saturday once a week. And he was only 21 right now. And life was, of course, meant to be lived in these tiny compartments of frivolity and youth, temperance and age. Literature and seriousness. Aspiration and reality. Sex and the thought of more sex to come.

This incident of Lambert forfeiting any real concern for his poetry (he didn't even pause or change his expression when his sexy cohorts interrupted his glory with tales of nothingness) had troubled Carrigan deeply for some time (it was a good poem and not at all about clouds or sunsets or springtime or youth or death or loss or regret; Carrigan had read it three full times when *The Review* came out), but as the 8:00 pm bells faded out this night, Carrigan developed a new sense of resolve—"But I'm advanced," he said aloud to no one in particular. "My flame-outs still matter."

There was no sarcasm in his voice, and a mounting seriousness of purpose made squints out of his hard, unusually bright green eyes as he pulled his grey coat on and buried his slumped neck under the upturned collar. He marched in loud, almost thunderous steps with his hands in his pockets and his head projected down enough to see the cracks in his worn brown shoes as he descended a fragile wooden staircase towards the frigid early November air. It seemed only right that if he would give into distraction, he would do it with resolve and pace and authority. His integrity (in a literary sense at least) was going to remain beyond reproach.

They had deemed this night a mega moon, or super moon event—an instance where the moon was as large and as luminous as it could ever be. Carrigan found this fitting to the prospect of creation, but when he reached the street and swiveled his head around in a complete circle and still couldn't even find a glimmer of the moon, he jeered himself and almost gave in to the idea that nature was conspiring against him. The idea struck him as an obnoxiously self-important one, but he figured it wouldn't be so bad just as long as he didn't say it out loud or to anyone else. And it seemed like if he really was to be an "advanced" writer whose flameouts still mattered and whose projects were more essential than intramural volleyball (which was a genuine statement, as Carrigan loved intramural volleyball), then some self-importance was going to be an abject necessity.

As he was mulling over whether or not he had transitioned away from the ironic use of the term "advanced," the bells chimed in that it was now 9:00. A full hour spent contemplating the nature of his literary presence and persona without actually writing a single word, but that seemed a writer-type thing to do as well. His futility was a kind of badge of honor—anyone could write a lot of pages if the words were like a grocery list or a birthday card. No, the absence of words on Carrigan's page was proof-positive that he had the greatness—and for a moment, he considered turning in a completely blank page to prove that he revered the craft more than the rest of them—clearly more than his 13 "advanced" colleagues in Mowbray's creative fiction course, who would most likely write something about their grandfathers to represent man's attachment to history and family no matter the pain of it all, or their closeness to their dogs as a facile hint of the alienation that people feel for people when free-will and the ability to argue back is involved, or some *Stand by Me* abomination about runaways coming of age, or groups of mismatched kids bonding in the summertime, or even some half-hearted Poe rip-off that pretended to be a riveting mystery story but was just formulaic tripe that they parroted from a crime show they fell asleep watching the night before. Either way, it was all plot. It was all story, story, story. Where were the beautiful sentences that were a story in themselves because they had pathos and a vagueness of reference? Where was the mourning of their absence? And when did disdain for them arise—

"John, your language overwhelms your plot."

"John, this piece seems to be entirely about its words."

"John, I need to find out where these people met, and I need to know some specifics about this day, and a back story about why she's riding a train and how long they've been together and what their issues are."

"Stop being such an asshole," he admonished himself in a terse whisper. And he actually liked most of the stories he read in Mowbray's workshop (the professor with the enticingly valorous literary name.

Carrigan had envisioned him coming to class in a waistcoat and a sheathed dagger before the semester started), or at least, found aspects within the dredge and dispassionate malaise of it all that he liked quite a lot, and those tiny aspects redeemed all the dredge in a way. Yes, he was a fan of literature—an unadulterated one at that.

"A blank page?" Carrigan audibly snickered at how insufferable he could be when he really wanted to, or that is, when he didn't care to stop himself. In fact, not only was Carrigan's page blank, but as the bells completed their 9:00 pm announcement, and as a five-minute sojourn out to the street became an hour-long speculation, Carrigan actually felt duty-bound to retract a line he had scribbled on a napkin some hours before. It read,"The immoral alacrity of all human history, and the brutish sluggishness of a single day's time."

Permeating and unyielding cloud-cover was the culprit in the failure of the mega moon event. Carrigan figured you couldn't blame the moon for that. "We can only be what we be," he thought. "And the powers that be do what they do." The two actions seemed wholly and frighteningly independent—it was like the absence of justice within entities that you couldn't even blame for their prejudice or self-interest or nepotism. It was just a visceral absence of justice with no sniveling tyrant or whining malcontent to pin it on. Complaining made it feel alright; this was the absence of complaint.

The bells aggressively rang their 10:00 pm song as Carrigan pulled out his notepad and wrote his first line—"We don't even get to be righteously angry when the moon fails us; we are all small."

Carrigan quickly scratched this line out too—this wasn't fiction; it was epigram, and not so good epigram at that.

There was some remote flickering light in the grey November darkness, and it was man-made, and coming from three students sitting together on the Woolsey Hall front steps typing on laptops. Carrigan had started to notice this phenomenon more and more; some people were even bringing these things to classes in place of their usual notebooks, or their usual nothing. It seemed like the beginning of something, or the end of something else. Maybe that was what New Haven was. Or what America was. Carrigan was sure that the world had changed more in the last century than it had during the previous nine. He looked back at the three young and enthusiastic laptop users, now laughing to each other as they pointed at something happening on one of the computer screens, and he suddenly knew what he wanted to write a scene about.

It is agonizing for a man to live in a place with no history—to have nothing to rebel against, to have no understanding of his own depth and size, broadness and inadequacy. New Haven had a kind of history in that it was connected to other kinds of histories and attitudes that visited if not always remained—through Yale, through the Revolutionary War where one overgrown, bloated, wondrously accomplished, gallingly unfair, religiously treacherous, literarily genius, and self-entitled nation became two middling, confused and ideologically non-descript nations, and through the assorted assemblage of people that walked through it from time to time.

Carrigan thought of Fitzgerald and nothing else at this moment. He was a perfect conjuration of this thought of the history of other histories. He was always about the past and always in the new. He was both Irish and American. He was both always in love and always reflective about its leaving.

And now Carrigan considered the immense likelihood that Fitzgerald had visited New Haven with his wife Zelda in the fall of 1931 for the Yale-Princeton game, right after "Babylon Revisited" had been printed in the *Saturday Evening Post.* It seemed only probable that Scott Fitzgerald would be searching for something of the past in '31, and more likely something of his student-hood of the teens and not the ubiquitous successes and excesses of the '20's. That was descript and portrayed in motion pictures and had become a brand name, actually several brand names. But the college years were always about becoming instead of being, and even the faintest remembrance of that atmosphere must have been welcomed in '31. Fitzgerald had so poignantly brokered the clear divide between romanticism and sentimentalism—had so vividly exposed sentimentality as the wretched forfeiture of verve and life that it was; a moribund and decrepit belief that the best time in life was always sometime before—Monsignor Darcy had told Amory Blaine and Nick had tried to tell Gatsby. Carrigan could palpably feel the wrenching conflict that must have been invading Fitzgerald's psyche in 1931, while home from Paris and visiting the ghosts of the past. It wasn't so much a retreat towards sentimentality, but sentimentality for romanticism that would've driven him to New Haven in the year that "Babylon" was printed, with Zelda, who had been the essential vagueness of a mighty dream, and now the texture of his throbbing reality.

As the bells projected their midnight reverie, Carrigan made it back up the creaking wooden stairs, ripped off his grey coat, sat back down at his desk with pen in his right hand and with his left hand running through his still sweaty hair. He figured he'd write it in the likeness of the Amory and Rosalind departure scene from *This Side of Paradise.* That seemed only appropriate given his instant obsession with things that were coming, going, and resonating all at the same time. He started brusquely, and did not quit until he was done:

It was the 10th of November, 1931, and Scott Fitzgerald walked up College Street quickly, but not quickly enough to catch up to Zelda who anxiously walked ahead of him, furiously and disgustedly moaning every time her tilted black hat failed to stop the cold autumn rain from extinguishing her cigarette. Princeton had just gotten trounced 51-14 by Yale and Zelda was traversing the far north side of the New Haven Green in search of a suitable restaurant. She settled on Randolph's and held the door for Scott, his ashen face finally showing some subtle cracks of age under his eyes, some cracks in an eternal youth that had only made him weary, as he lived in the autumn of his 35th year. His soft brown hair was parted down the middle, and the sides flayed out wildly as the rain started to drain from his scalp and its dampness washed away his hair treatment. They sat at a middle table, at Zelda's insistence, and both ordered scotch, soda and coffee.

Zelda: Are you having fun yet Scott? Have you found whatever it is you're looking for in this dreadful borough? I swear these prep school towns are all the same—gothic buildings and navy-blue pinstriped ties and modern chants meant to sound ancient and boys that are all handsome in exactly the same way. I'd beg you to go back to Paris but they've completely overtaken that place too (in making this remark, she waved her left hand caustically at several tables filled with Yale and Princeton alums sitting near the door of the restaurant). You know, if I were a man I could've done pretty goddamn well here, Scott, or at least made a hell of a row in the process. And I wouldn't have gotten caught up in this dining club rubbish and newspaper competition. Oh, maybe I would've, who's to say? (She had lighted a new cigarette and her energy seemed to perk with its ignition). What a hopeless tragedy it was that they left these sanctuaries of intellectual prowess to all you little automatons with the same fashion sense and the same marginally bohemian mothers who told you to be yourselves, but not at too much expense to your standing. (Scott forced a quick, sad smile and nodded with his lips pursed). Oh, don't you go being quiet on me now, Scott. You're insufferable when you're quiet. Be sad all you want, but just don't do it quietly, for my sake. Entertain me at the very least. I do miss your passionate little fusses. Your St. Paul obstinacies. I figured, if nothing else, this trip back before the war might muster up one of those.

Scott: You haven't told me what you think of "Babylon," Zelda. I've been a bit worried about how you might take it. I hope you can see that it's a love letter to what I want for us—an apology for all the blindness, for all the nights that were wasted, a celebration of what we can be and not a lament on what we weren't.

Zelda: I shouldn't have asked you to talk.

Scott: I'm serious. I know it must have been a bit harsh that the Helen character was dead, but you're not dead Zelda, and we can have what Charlie and Helen had lost.

Zelda: Yes, I can interpret just fine. Save your pedantic, facile literary explanations for someone else. I get imagery you know—and my own stuff is pretty damned good. Yes, Scott, I get it, just because the wife in the story is dead doesn't mean I think you view me as already dead in any kind of symbolic or pressing way—at least I didn't until we engaged in this engrossing conversation (Zelda rolled her neck dramatically and looked to the ceiling of the restaurant). Where does all of this personal precaution come from anyway? I've been morphed into dozens of horrible little wretches in your works before.

Scott: I don't know. I'm just curious as to what you think about this one. It's so much different than my other stuff. I don't know.

Zelda: I think "The Saturday Evening Post" should print my stuff. (Scott was visibly frustrated but didn't want to sigh or shorten his tone).

Scott: Anything else?

Zelda: I hate Charlie Wales.

Scott: Oh, that's okay (He breathed deeply, and almost seemed relieved). He's supposed to be ambivalently interpreted; he's supposed to allow the reader to choose between his treachery and self-immolation, and his humane, small heroism.

Zelda: None of that has anything to do with why I hate him.

Scott: Oh?

Zelda: He's a bore, Scotty. A dreadful one.

Scott: He's not meant to be grand.

Zelda: We're all meant to be grand. We're only not when little guilt-ridden self-crucifiers like yourself rob it from us. And the critics will now rave about your evolution, your maturity. But I see you dead in this rain, Scott Fitzgerald. (She became very self-satisfied at her perfectly timed reference and called the waiter over in an act of apparent triumph.) I'm ready to order, and let's have something hearty—butternut squash and full serving chicken sandwich on a roll.

Scott: Just the frog leg appetizer, please (he was visibly forlorn, and his small order was a kind of resignation to the failing glory of the day).

Zelda: The Princeton delight. How appropriate for a man who has lost his way. At least you can sense that something is missing, my darling. There you go with that rumpled little face, bitterly mad at me and too in love to walk away. I miss you, Scotty.

Scott: I miss you, too.

Zelda: No you don't. I never changed. You miss loving Zelda Sayre. But you're the only one who ever left or returned. I just changed my name. I mean, since when did you dread the sadness; since when did you resent the absence? I married an artist, Scott, and I don't regret it—your guilt is misplaced. Your guilt is what you should feel guilty for.

(Scott felt dizzy and sipped his water voraciously. He turned his head sharply right to look out at the Green but the windows were clouded with condensation, and the Green shrouded in rising fog. He was boxed in, and Zelda's hard, angular face and piercing blue eyes couldn't be avoided. Just then, Thomas Park D'Invillers, the poet and Scott's beloved Princeton roommate, walked by their table and put his hand on Scott's shoulder. He was a smallish, shy man, wearing a brown corduroy coat over his deep orange Princeton sweater with the "P" emblazoned in large black stitching on the front. Scott rose instinctively and hugged him, a full-bodied hug that lasted at least three beats longer than Thomas Park D'Invillers would've expected.)

Tom: I've been looking for you Scott—this is the third restaurant I've been in, searching around for a befuddled man with stern eyes and a coat that was just a hint too short.

Zelda: Wonderful! The reclusive Thomas Park D'Invillers—the only person in the world who can make my husband feel worse about himself than I do.

Scott: She's kidding, Tom.

Zelda: I certainly am not.

Scott: Well, she means it as a compliment.

Zelda: This is at least a partial truth. You see Tom, he's always felt morbidly guilty that he was more famous than you—Tom, a better writer, a better sort, more genuine, more humble, more loving and giving, and completely unconcerned with the fact that no one has any idea who he is. (Tom demurred. He initiated a close-lipped half smile, but did not laugh. It was only too clear that he agreed with what Zelda had said. But he loved Scott purely and actually envied his precociousness and grandiosity, at times. Scott's belief that the world cared, or even could care for and be mutilated or redeemed by the things he had to say, for the pictures he had to paint, was certainly something to be admired, almost yearned for. But yes, Tom was a better sort—he still revered his own words even when nobody read them.)

Tom: That's sweet of you, Zelda. Really it is.

Zelda: Don't misunderstand me Tom—I could take or leave most of your stuff. But my husband here is just mad about it—a real sycophant, you know. He thinks you're his conscience, and he feels so often estranged from you.

Scott: She's got me there, old friend. Are you writing?

Tom: Now and again. How's Scottie?

Scott: Ten years old and smarter than all of us, Tom. And no pretense, no vanity. An actual happy one.

Zelda: Her teachers are absurd.

Scott: They're sweet. They're just simple.

Zelda: Oh, they're not so harmless. All they care about is how straight the bow in her hair is, and does it match her dress, and "why, what wonderful manners she has." (She dragged deeply on her cigarette). I know she's succeeding every time they make a disconcerting frown at her. (She perked up again, with mischief in her eyes). Say Tom, what did you make of "Babylon?"

Tom: Deeply melancholy, and riveting. I could picture our old boy tapping at the keys with genuine distress. I was really proud of him for sending something in without bells or whistles. (Scott grabbed Tom's shoulder affectionately and tapped it repeatedly while chuckling heartily).

Zelda: Your hair has gone quite grey, Tom. (His temples were a deep, stone grey—not a transitioning grey, but the end of something that came before).

Tom: (laughing) I suppose we've all grown a bit older, a bit wearier. I don't know—I think I finally actually look like myself. (They all laughed now, Zelda somewhat sardonically, but not entirely. It was clear that she loved Tom too; she never would've bothered to desecrate him if not—she was reserving her righteous energy for special occasions these days. The thirties seemed a wholly new time—a time for conservation.)

Zelda: Do you boys remember when I first met Tom?

Scott: I was writing ad-copy in New York, and Tom and I were living in that closet. Well, I had a job writing ad-copy, but I didn't write too much of it. Or that is, I wrote literary ad-copy and they didn't print it.

Tom: I remember. Always. It was, shall we say, a time of transition? A time of engaging tumult that yields worthy result?

Zelda: Don't be polite, Thomas. We're all family here. I met you the day I left Scott—the day I cancelled our engagement for the first time. The day I told him, in front of his beloved Thomas Parke D'Invillers, that he was a failure who would only trap me in a small place with no colors. Oh, you must have found me such a wretch.

Tom: I remember how much you loved him. I remember how hard you tried to pretend that it didn't bother you to go—to make it easier on Scott. I remember, my dear Zelda. You're not really much of an actress, when it comes down to it.

Zelda: You find me better than I find myself.

Tom: And what happened the following spring?

Zelda: They printed his book.

Tom: They printed his book.

Zelda: And I came back.

Tom: You were always coming back.

Zelda: You think so?

Scott: A bystander in my own life once again.

Tom: I'm sorry, Francis. (Tom laughed). This is the most I've talked in months. It seems as if I've gotten carried away.

(Just then, a small brass band roared up in the left corner of the dining room. They were a group of blustery old alums from the '80's with similar wavy white hair and all wearing the same sweater as Tom. They were playing some rousing tune from the '20's and the whole assemblage, and their counterfeit of happiness, seemed out of

place).

I think that's my cue.

Scott: Ours too, old boy.

(Zelda stood first and kissed Tom warmly on the cheek, running her fingers through the close-cropped grey hair on his temples).

Scott: You'll write me, Tom?

Tom: Yes. And goodbye Zelda. And you'll be writing Scott?

Scott: I just might. Goodbye, old man.

(Scott held the door for Zelda and they exited Randolph's and entered a driving rain. Scott propped open a black umbrella with a silver handle and Zelda took his arm and pressed her lips softly against his ashen cheek. They walked north, away from the Green.)

Zelda: Do you remember the first time that we were here together?

Scott: Yes, darling. 1917. I was a mess.

Zelda: You had just failed math for the first time, and they were going to take your spot on the "Princetonian" away and you thought that was just about it for you. "A bright light extinguished before the dawn." I think that was it (she laughed playfully). Was I more beautiful then?

Scott: No.

Zelda: Were we better then?

Scott: I'm not so sure.

Carrigan pumped his right fist in glory. He breathed deeply through his nose and exalted at the ceiling. The bells were ringing. 7:00 am. It was the first chime he had noticed since midnight. He stepped into a warm and bracing shower that he had just enough time for.

At 7:45, Carrigan pulled on a grey pair of Dockers and buttoned a white oxford shirt. He tossed his coat over his buoyant shoulders and slipped a navy blue knit cap on over his wet, matted-down hair. It was a ten-minute walk to Mowbray's class, and he did not want to be late. Not today.

He dropped his scene on Mowbray's lectern as he bounced through the door. He listened to Mowbray philosophize on Keats for a full six minutes before he stood up and left, as if to use the bathroom. But he did not return. Not this day.

He walked in a misting November rain towards College Street, full of both righteous energy and that uniquely narcotic energy that accompanies moments of the greatest exhaustion. He walked into Randolph's and sat by the window as the half chime signified 8:30 am. He closed his eyes deeply and with forehead leaning backwards, a close-lipped smile engulfing his face. He had imagined something. Something that wasn't there was now there. He was "advanced."

Quickly he checked himself—realizing that he had "imagined" something about people that had lived, that had themselves acted—that had themselves supplied the pretext and context.

Carrigan sat sullenly with his fist in his cheek, until he noticed a young girl, maybe a sophomore, reading a haggard copy of *Macbeth* at the table diagonally to his left. Carrigan was virtually overjoyed.

Macbeth, or some variation of him, had lived. So had Coriolanus and Hamlet, never mind the goddamn history plays—the "Julius Caesar's," the "Antony and Cleopatra's." They were borderline children's stories by the time Shakespeare had gotten around to them. Things seemed in a rightful order again.

Carrigan retrieved a leaky pen from the interior of his grey coat. He scribbled a note on a smoothed napkin: "One person lives. The next one writes about him. The next one writes about the writer." It all seemed all right—this assumption of power and influence followed by a forfeiture of that power and influence and self-identification. It was all creation. It was all existing in a kind of artistic real-time. It was all made illuminant by those who bothered to articulate it. And all transfigured by those who cared to articulate it in beautiful, syrupy segments of prose. He would give the people what they wanted from time to time—give them some people talking to each other. He owed it to them; he was powerless without them. They were nonexistent without him.

Carrigan looked through the glass window now and saw a vibrant and bustling Green through the quickening mist. He was "advanced." And he was fine with it. He headed back to his room, a cheese danish dangling from his mouth as he held his hat in one hand and pulled his coat on with the other. He went quickly to sleep, removing only his shoes as he climbed into his bed.

He woke an hour later—fending off nightmares about the word "original." The individual letters of the word were advancing towards his head like rogue or kamikaze aircraft, and deftly and easily eluding him when he tried to smother them in his hand. They kept returning and returning and returning—so unafraid of him, and so elusive. The letters took vivid colors and shapes, but the backdrop of the dream was a nondescript black—shapeless and without even walls for the purpose of framing, or doors or windows for the purpose of escape. There was no television to distract, no woman for succor and comfort—no one to cry to. No father to benignly lie to him. No Professor Keating to promise him a greatness that he himself had not obtained.

He felt oppressively nauseated, and he hoped the cheese danish had just gone bad. Carrigan rooted around in the trash for the label, but stopped, realizing he really didn't want to know if it was past it's sell-by date. He picked up his basketball and dribbled to the park in the slushy rain. His hands picking up cakes of sooty filth. His eyes burning paradoxically as they endured the sharp anguish of the cold, dirty rain. The fall had seemed to come and go already. But this wasn't quite winter either.

NOVEMBER 12, 2000

There were two things worth noting about Carrigan's Modern European History professor, or at least two things that Carrigan would remember each day he saw him. Professor Timothy Sherman had a strange habit of beginning an inordinate amount of sentences with the phrase, "The thing about the Nazis was…"

It was probably just a quirk of speech or an unconscious habit picked up long ago, but nonetheless its implication always troubled Carrrigan; as if the Nazis were just like anybody else in virtually all discernible ways, just like any other random assemblage of Girl Scouts or bowling enthusiasts or Civil War re-enactors, but that they just had this one little personality nuance or philosophical tenet that made all the difference. Carrigan was sure that nobody else in the room ever thought twice about this, but the inference embedded in Professor Sherman's semantic repetition gave Carrigan great and continuous pause; there just had to be something greater dividing the Nazis from the 12 year-old-girl who sold him over-priced Samoas outside of the grocery store than some singular personality trait or momentary obsession—it had to be more complex, more engrossing, more far-reaching and consuming and premeditated and concerted—each thing connecting to a web of other things, at the very least—than just some random and independent quirk of birth or transitory cultural influence. Now yes, Sherman would often finish his troubling preface with varying endings to the clause, so when taken in totality, he didn't necessarily seem to be arguing that there was just *one* thing about the Nazis. Or, maybe, he was arguing for just one single identifier of difference, and was simply changing his mind about what that little thing was all the time. Either way, Carrigan saw it as a distinctly flawed way of thinking, or, a persistently flawed way of speaking, which to Carrigan was just as bad if not worse.

The other thing worth mentioning about Carrigan's Modern European History professor was more personal, though, oddly enough, much vaguer. Professor Timothy Sherman looked exactly like Carrigan's father. But the word exact is strange, and perhaps inappropriate here, for Carrrigan never really possessed a distinctive portrait of his father in his psyche. Every memory featured a confused group of others standing in the way, or a panorama of distraction, or an opaque shadow, and none of these images stayed in one place long enough to be interpreted or deconstructed. So more accurately, 45-year-old Timothy Sherman remarkably resembled the assembled collage of fleeting images that Carrigan had of his father—he was an incredible representation of a composite character largely concocted by art and license and the passage of time.

Carrigan's father was a composite, an amalgam of vagaries, not just in looks (always non-descript words—handsome, tall) but in personality (flashes of charm, stoic, fierce, Irish—which was perhaps the vaguest of the vague, but perhaps not) and even in action and deed; he "knew" Bobby Sands. He was "around" when Lord Mountbatten was killed. He had twice "competed" in the British open.

Even upon coming to America, which is the only context in which John ever knew him until his funeral, the ambivalent kaleidoscope continued. When he asked his mother what his father did for work, she answered,

"He works in an office."

And this seemed ill-fitting and ill-suited to the wild brace of his eyes. When asked who he worked with the answer was similar,

"Lovely people; your father likes them very much. He's never been happier."

He had connection to so many things, but intimacy with almost none, and this was exactly how John remembered him—quick flashes of rage that were extinguished just as quickly (did he feel he didn't have the right to be angry? He was a Catholic after all, and so guilt was always adjacent), moments of pure charm and easy humor that he never seemed energized enough to sustain, and seeming epochs of ambiguous silence.

John was nine years old when his father died, or when he was killed, depending on who you talk to. It was an "accident." What an epic word that is—accident—a word to cover all manner of sin, including vanity, and, a word abdicating the blame from both mortal sin and vanity. He thought again about the cacophony of story proffered to him around the time of his father's death, and by the anonymous blokes with the fervor, passion, and whiskey at the funeral, or wake, to be exactly accurate.

When women told him it was an accident, they had rubbed his head, knelt down to eye-level and offered him a cookie or a brownie. When men told him it was an accident, they did it with a wink, and a nod of the head. So maybe he had been killed by the British police, or maybe he was just as pedestrian as every other nobody who falls off the face of the earth before they've lived a natural time. Maybe he turned left on red and hit a bus. Maybe he was eating an ice-cream cone by the Liffey and fell over the barrier when it started to slip from his grasp. Or maybe his death really was an assassination, like Kiernan's had been—his throat slit by an Ulsterman after he refused to snitch about an operation, or poisoned in a basement after saying something too bold or manifest. John Carrigan knew that he would never know for sure, because it was just as likely that people would lie to cover a pedestrian death, as they would a fantastic one. And while many Irishmen are unflinchingly loyal to things like the church, or their wives, or literature, or football, or whiskey, or a countless myriad more of individualized and impossible to name things, myth was the only thing that every Irishman was loyal to. And in fairness, this didn't bother John at all, as life wasn't really anything without the dynamism of embellishment, the liberty of imagination and poetry—the redeeming power of lying.

John would've liked to know whether the lies told about his father gave cover to the man's enemies, or to his friends. It wasn't an obsessive desire, however, but just a passing, almost recreational curiosity that Carrigan picked back up from time to time, like his golf clubs when the last snow melts, or a board game one might stumble across looking for something else, and at least for an afternoon forget why it had been tossed under the couch in a basement that was never visited anymore.

But on this day, November 12, 2000, John Carrrigan's father would've turned 50 years old. And he sat in Modern European History with Professor Timothy Sherman, who looked so much like the best designed composite of his father, and spoke in that disconcertingly inexact way that was all too familiar, and he thought about him. Or more specifically, Carrigan speculated about his father, as that was all that could really ever be done concerning a man of which he had no real knowledge of where he was born, and no real memory of where he had been buried.

Carrigan's father's absence had made him feel empty quite often, but he couldn't say it made him feel sad, per se. He felt a deep secondary sadness every time he saw sadness creep into his mother's eyes, but he could never actually be sure that her sorrow had anything to do with the death of her husband, and he never had the urge to ask.

The truth was, that there were even times when John Carrigan felt relieved not to be burdened with a father, not because he harbored any particular cruelty or ill-feeling towards his own, but because, relatively, he often observed the damage that other fathers would do—overcheering or too tragic sadness at Little League games that made the world seem only as big as Little League itself; imbroglios over skipped classes or missed homework or shoes left on the couch or televisions played too loudly; family routines and planned vacations and itinerary on the refrigerator. There was no greatness in lives lived so domestically; he had gleaned that from his father—even while alive, and he was thankful for it. And in death his father could be anything now; he could even be the kind of man who couldn't let him down.

Paternal speculation lingered as Carrigan meandered slowly to his next class, which was 19th Century Poetry. The professor was an aged, tiny Polish woman, who despite her age was doggedly buoyant in her movements about the classroom, and had retained the brightness in her luminous green eyes—eyes that appeared to be virtually neon when she became overtly passionate, which was quite often. Dr. Agnes Vladnowitz was a woman fated to survive, that is to say, she was a tough woman to kill. She had survived one plane crash, shown up late and missed another flight that ended up going down in the North Sea, and as her students could witness every time she rolled her sleeves up when the temperature grew warm or when she worked herself into a particular vigor, she bore the faded, yet permanently inked numerical calling card of her time at Buchenwald on her left forearm; Carrigan often wondered what she thought the "thing about the Nazis was." But the truth was, it seemed like she didn't think there was anything at all about them.

She never once did voluntarily talk about the war or her own experience in it. A particularly bold student asked her one day why she never mentions it.

"Because the Nazis aren't worthy of study," she said, as if responding like an answering machine message to a phone call she had no interest at all in picking up, from a caller she had no interest at all in indulging.

The bold undergraduate continued her line of inquiry—"Respectively, Dr. Vladnowitz, how can you say that? How can you even think to say that? The party responsible for the end of Old Europe, for 50 million deaths, for virulence and disease and unholy experimentation and incalculable suffering and destruction of property and art and history and culture. I know I sound awful disagreeing with someone who was there, but this is a university, and how can you say that such an entity is not worthy of study—how can we ignore such a pestilence?"

The Polish professor's response was composed and arrived without hesitation.

"What do you do with a rabid dog?"

"Excuse me," said the undergraduate, "I don't follow your reference."

"If a rabid dog wanders onto your street do you study it, do you seek to explain it, do you give it justification by engaging in discourse?"

"Respectively, one is an animal with no consciousness."

"Which one?"

"Okay Dr. Vladnowitz, we'll have to agree to disagree." The undergraduate was a lithe, attractive blonde girl whose tips of her hair were becoming dirty with perspiration.

"But what do you do with the dog?"

"I suppose you put it down."

"You put it down."

"And if it kills you and everyone you love before you can put it down?'

"Then you mourn your dead, and live on after the funerals—you create and exist."

"I understand, Dr. Vladowtitz."

"Don't get me wrong, young lady—you do come to learn, to be aware of the signs pointing to when more rabid dogs may be advancing on your territory, and remembering your past degradation, and learning the lessons of prior incursions, you react with alacrity and assuredness and righteousness, but those are all sensate reactions and you store them in the recesses of your muscles and your tissues, but in the interim, you never give them your heart or your mind."

"Yes ma'am," said the pretty, suddenly cow-towed undergraduate. It was the only thing Dr. Agnes Vladnowitz ever said about Nazi Germany, or occupied Europe for that matter—Carrigan felt is sufficed, though his own fascination on the subject was unquenchable.

Carrigan was purely enraptured with Dr. Agnes Vladnowitz, a pure affection not muddled by sexual desire or egotistical intellectual rivalry. She was always dramatic, always historical, and yet always entertaining, which was exactly what Carrigan thought a professor should be. He enjoyed being there; her class was an escape and a pertinent reality all at once, but today, everything seemed in reference to his father, and it was daunting and wholly unexpected—he didn't think of his father often, either overtly or subconsciously. He was a different person when he knew his father after all, but all of that delayed or procrastinated speculation that he assumed he was supposed to encounter was coming today, all at once, like some essay that you refuse to do in stages and then let consume every breath, or some craving that is denied and then indulged with the voraciousness of an addict diving and fumbling for his needle.

It was everywhere, consuming his psyche and his reference. Dr. Vladnowitz had lived through the inevitable demise associated with both aviation failure and the inhumanity of the concentration camps. She hadn't survived one of them; she had survived two things that no one in the mortal sphere ever seriously came out of. She was just supposed to be alive, it seemed. Carrigan's father's life was innocuous, or more accurately, mysterious, and his death seemed inevitable. Carrigan quickly thought back to the funeral, the images of which he remembered distinctly, virtually photographically—a number of people did seem sad (genuine tears and instinctual gestures; even as a boy Carrigan could read affect) but as he thought of it today, no one seemed surprised. In truth, at the time, it was the only funeral that Carrigan had ever been to, and so he had no frame of reference for the presence of surprise at such an event, but still, it was distinct—no one seemed surprised. Carrigan wondered if his father was just one of those people who were supposed to be dead, and if there were such a thing as people who were just supposed to be dead. He wondered how much control his father had had in becoming one of those people, and the balance between God and the individual and if some people exist simply as balance or perspective for others who become descript by sheer virtue of being different from those who are fated to be dead. As always, he thought of his father in the abstract. Dr. Agnes Vladnowitz had stories and wounds and presence. She was so very descript. She was everything Carrigan's father was not.

As the clock chimed three, Carrigan ambled out of the room searching his psyche for something tangible to describe his father that could be stored in his memory and revisited at random and urbane moments of happenstance and conversation. The effect was striking, not so much for the peculiarity of such a desire, but because it was absolutely the first time Carrigan had ever felt such an impulse; his father had always rushed into his mind when confronted with portraits or mosaics of what he was not, or more accurately, what Carrigan couldn't be sure he was or was not. These moments always galvanized philosophical inquiry, but today inquiry wasn't good enough. Carrigan needed something—an IT as D.H. Lawrence might call it, but even less inscrutable. Understanding his father meant nothing, and worse than that it seemed detached and wretched; he suddenly wanted to love him, and love him in a more raw and less admiring way than he loved his 72-year-old 19th Century Poetry professor with the inspiring countenance and the visible scars of Buchenwald, and who was always so shockingly unaware of her own devastation.

Understanding is an anathema to love, for one can never really love those he understands, as it's too clinical, too diminishing to claim to "get someone." Love is the suspension of analysis, and willful hypocrisy of judgment that is motivated by instinct and emotional craving, and is expressed by extrapolating isolated moments and letting them stand in for the entirety of identity, or, at least, this was the one rendering of love in which Carrigan could hope to love his father, and so today, he yearned for it, yearned to at least attempt it, and he besieged his memory, which was other worldly by nature but shadowy when it came to his father, to find singular moments of shared experience or message. After an hour of sitting in solace, he had found three.

SUNSET—NOVEMBER 12, 2000

Carrigan found three messages quite literally—in a journal given to him by his mother when he migrated from campus back home (why did his dorm suddenly not feel like home?) after 19th Century Poetry.

"Has anyone else seen this?"

"No," his mother said succinctly and without explanation. She was a stylish and beautiful (the adjective was simplistic and often too easily ascribed but was nothing short of pinpoint and deserving here) woman of 45. She wore a crimson Ralph Lauren pullover sweater over an upturned white golf shirt and dark blue jeans, her black hair falling to shoulder's length and speckled evenly with grey throughout. She was drinking a cup of tea, and as always, holding the mug caressingly in both hands, as if there were a persistent chill in the air, even indoors. She had a habit of looking like a background figure on the cover photo of a prep school catalogue, casually watching on at a soccer game on a crisp, autumn New England day infused with amber, perfectly outfitted for that last outdoor day before the azure campus would be blanketed with snow and melt indistinguishably into the backdrop of the hundreds of fall seasons that had already come and gone at pastoral New England academic settings.

"How could you keep this from us?" Carrigan asked with some force but in a voice mostly devoid of anger.

"I haven't read it myself. I figured it was just as likely devastating as it was likely to produce joy or solace or conciliation."

"So why today?"

"Today was the first day you ever asked."

"Do you want to look at it with me?"

"Are you sure you even want to?" Emily Mary Carrigan retorted with a modicum of rancor.

"I don't know," John Carrigan said abruptly.

"But you're going to anyway."

"Yeah. Blind allegiance to random impetuosity and instinct is sort of my thing. It kind of eats me up."

"I understand."

"So, do you want me to tell you what's in it?"

"Just read," his mother said soothingly. "Tell me whatever you'd like to when you're done."

"Ok, Mom."

"And I'll listen to whatever I'd like to."

"Ok, Mom."

"You're 21 years old, John."

"This is true, but I'm assuming that's the beginning of a point and not the entirety of what you want to say. Lay it on me. It's been a familial kind of day—I can handle it Mom."

"I just mean you don't have to figure everything out right now. You don't need answers to every question. What would you even do with the rest of your life if you found them besides be painfully bored?"

"I know that, Mom. I do. I'm not trying to find every answer. But I mean, I need a base of knowledge and understanding if I'm ever going to get anything useful out of these flashes of enlightenment that are going to arrive in natural time. It would be kind of a tragedy if I experienced one and didn't know how to process it."

Emily Carrigan smiled wryly. It was both comforting and frustrating to have a son who was smarter than her. He was really a sweet boy—emotional, philosophical, timid, but the fears she encountered in the aftermath of his almost mythic spelling bee flameout remained. She wondered if his brilliance made him colder, made him a little more scornful of everyone else, and a little too fascinated with the select few that could hold his attention for more than a fleeting instance.

"How's Jane?"

"I bet she's fine."

"John."

"What was that about not having to figure things out or have solidified answers?"

"She's not a thing, John, not some entity."

"Circumstances might ebb and flow but the feeling remains and if worth it, that can be recaptured."

"You're a lovely boy, John—more than just a little bit handsome, but you don't think she may have other feelings too? May just bump into them walking down sidewalks that you're avoiding?"

John may have been smarter than her, but Emily Carrigan was not exactly stupid, and she was certainly wiser than this son.

"You didn't leave. And he was always gone. I remember that much."

"He died when I was 33, John."

"I know."

"Who knows if I was done coming or going yet?"

"I understand."

"I love you, John."

"I love you too, Mom."

Still unsure of whether or not his mother had actually already read the journal herself (she was an authentic woman but did live in a family that found benign lying to be a form of both grace and artistic indulgence), Carrigan retreated to his childhood bedroom, the walls still adorned with posters of Red Sox shortstop Nomar Garciapara and Michael Jordan, and a map of county Galway that his father had pinned up when John was five or six years old.

"Why Galway?" Carrigan wondered aloud.

His funeral was in Dublin after all—was the map some kind of misdirection, or the only true clue in all the shadows and affect and resounding, unflinching death?

"One existential crisis at a time," he whispered, and opened the notebook.

To Carrigan's fascination, the journal wasn't so much a journal, but a series of tenets and discussions, supplemented by anecdotes and structured not unlike *Mediations* by Marcus Aurelius. And it was addressed to his children, as if he knew he would never be able to discuss these things in person (had he known that he was just one of those people who was fated to be dead?), or more cynically, just didn't want to, and writing some things down was a marginal means of doing penance.

Carrigan had never thought of his father as a philosophical man, but in fairness, he wasn't even sure of what his father had done for a living. There were three primary tenets addressed in the text, and each was infused with ample and sometimes rambling digression.

Money—I write about money first because it is what is valued by the largest number of people, and in turn, it is the prism in which people comprehend all else, and is most in need of being dispensed with. Now this is not Communistic or politically motivated—my objection to the predominance of money is not that it makes one corrupt or unjust, but that it makes one boring. Ambition fueled by the desire for money simplifies the individual—he begins to look through a pinhole and loses the ambling panorama and kaleidoscopic madness that greatness demands. Financial craving makes us hold an arbitrary line, and defames our wanderings and natural detours as shiftless and inexcusable lacks of direction and production. It only allows us to move forward, but greatness often circles back and very oft moves with crooked or jagged intent or purpose. In short, lives motivated and judged by accumulating money primarily move only one way, and life is only genuine when it meanders.

Carrigan stopped abruptly. "Genuine?" What a word. Carrigan sat back and pushed his long, delicate fingers against shut eyes, a shock of perspiring brown hair drifting over his left brow. John Carigan could produce a dozen arguments for legitimate ways that genuine behavior could be exhibited in any given situation or ethical quandary, but he realized quickly that he had no idea how to define the word in isolation. He was only a paragraph in, and already he felt uneasily closer to his dead father, who wrote so energetically, so abstractly, and so seemingly impersonally. John was confronted by the fact that the effect wasn't necessarily charming. He continued on, skipping some of the more dense paragraphs along the way.

But again, I have no politics in this—I'm not arguing for the abdication of money or advocating the start of a cohesive movement or endorsing moving out to the woods to escape the masses; I'm no Thoreau and I'm no Marx.....

John quickly speculated on who would've introduced his father to Thoreau or Marx. He pressed on.

Besides, starting a movement or escaping to the woods is weakness anyway, for it secures the power of capital by letting it galvanize your actions, just to the same effect as seeking it does ironically, if not more so. I'm reminded of what Faulkner said about nuclear fear, "Our tragedy today is a general and universal physical fear so long sustained by now that we can even bear it... The writer must teach himself that the basest of all things is to be afraid; and, teaching himself that, forget it forever, leaving no room in his workshop for anything but the old verities and truths of the heart, the old universal truths lacking which any story is ephemeral and doomed—love and honor and pity and pride and compassion and sacrifice."

John was startled—where had he picked up someone as insular as Faulkner? There were no books left in his old study downstairs (a damp basement cave that his mother referred to as a study), and no Faulkner volumes anywhere in the house other than his own closet, and those had been there only since the previous spring when John read *Light in August, As I lay Dying, and Go Down Moses* in Prof. Keating's class.

His father's solution for the saga of money was even more startling, however.

So just as Faulkner says about fear, I say about money—accept its existence, even its dominance on the psyche, and then forget it entirely—but with one caveat—always have a way to get it should its absence come to interfere with your other pursuits. I am not preaching for or endorsing any illegality—but there is a wonderful and vibrant middle ground between illegality and capital exhaustion.

The answer was a single word and at first John thought it was a joke, a moment of levity in a dense manifesto, but after reading on, not only did it become clear that it was not a joke, but actually an authentic and probably intended segue to the more human element of the journal, and in reading it, John felt all of his anxiety melt away; even if the rest was rubbish or heartbreaking or punishing, he was happy for the obsession that motivated his migration home on the day his father would've turned 50 years old had he not been one of those people who were just supposed to be dead.

Poker. Learn and master poker, and you will never go wanting, and you will never lose your soul.

John would smile every time he recalled it thereafter—it was an other-worldly, paternal note of acceptance and excusal for all the nights he was still not asleep when the dawn encroached—all those nights he was blurry-eyed but startlingly alert as he out-thought and out-lasted the two or three degenerates remaining in a back-room game, or the tourists too far behind to go upstairs and check into their rooms at a casino and face the accusatory stares of disappointment and disgust from their wives or girlfriends.

Dr. Agnes Vladnowitz had her airplane mishaps and a haunting and permanent reminder of Buchenwald on her frail, liver-spotted left forearm, but John and his father had disgustingly unjust river cards, and missed draws, and adrenaline-testing bluffs, and the humbling and crippling sorrow that accompanies the reoccurring and ever-present failure of such a pursuit. A kind of peace in the wild things, and someone with the same blood as him saw it the same way.

> *Don't confuse what I'm telling you with gambling; I don't want you to ever pull a slot machine or spin a roulette wheel or play blackjack or bet on a sports game—that's pure chance and it consumes you. Poker is remedy to that, a game of skill where talent and intellectualism and observation make you a winner, but still infused with the profound element of chance that strips you of total control and introduces injustice and an abject lack of fairness from time to time, and in some stretches, that lack of fairness is very frequent and almost debilitating.*
>
> *No, I don't want destruction and despair for my children, but I do want full spectrum humanity. We are mortal beings; we should not have perfection or invincibility, but we should be distinct from each other. That is exactly poker—differentiate yourself through verve and cunning and be receptive to the hardship that arrives again and again in a kind of natural rhythm, realizing that it does not last unless you give into it, unless you allow it to compromise your mind and weaken your spirit and vitality and stomach for the endeavor. And failing these compromises, it is an outlet for you to find money in the service of your identity instead. And failing these compromises when you lose, it is only money that you forfeit, which remember, I contend makes you boring and derivative anyway.*

John Carrigan smiled widely, even laughed audibly. It was circular and brilliant; serious and tongue-in-cheek all at once. It was academic but personal, because it was being written to and for him. Suddenly he could remember sitting around the kitchen table with his family, his father with a deck of cards in hand, asking them what were then incomprehensible questions about why they were making the decisions they were making—his mother smiling broadly, her hair still fully midnight black. This was how his father could interact—through the intermediary of ink or the pathos of a game of veritable chess that was embedded with both adrenaline and sadness and choice.

The rest of the section included some technical advice about tells and strategy (when a guy bets an indiscriminate amount, he's strong; when a guy moves all-in without pushing the chips in he's strong; when a guy says he'll show you his hand if you fold, he's weak, etc.) but all John focused on was the verve in his father's voice—that urging to push yourself into the realm of pure fear and vulnerability, while simultaneously maintaining the perspective that if all is lost, you lose nothing of value, only money. There was an exhilaration in that that John knew well, intimately well, and in an open page in the notebook, he began to write about a hand of Texas Hold'em he had played the night before:

I was in full control all evening—thinking two steps ahead of the table, keeping my composure, running the game. By 3:00 am there were only three other players left and two of them had announced they were leaving in the next orbit; there would only be a few more hands and I was up 1,500 dollars. I folded the next two hands and with one hand remaining I was dealt the 5/6 of diamonds. I raised and got one caller—the only player who had more chips than me, the only man who could ruin my evening. The flop came down—3 of diamonds, 4 of diamonds, and the 10 of clubs—a straight flush draw; I'm not there yet, but I love my hand, and I won't turn back. I can't. It would be undignified. It would be safe. It would have no poetry. My opponent is a mergers and acquisitions guy who thinks he can play but is fooled into that impression by the size of his bankroll—he can lose without financial pain so he takes reckless chances that appear like inspired zealotry but are actually much closer to empty bravado. He is first to act.

"It's late, kid," he murmurs out of the gruff of his five o'clock shadow that he'd be contractually required to shave before strolling into work the next morning. I felt sorry for him; he had no idea how pathetic his existence was.

"Yeah. So, what does that mean?" I ask with feigned irritation.

"It means, let's not fool around. I'll just end this now," he says caustically as he tosses two black chips causally into the pot—a 200 dollar bet.

I'd bet my self-respect that he's bluffing here and I can just raise and take the pot now. But I don't want that—I want it all. Not out of greed but out justice and fair competition. I decide to just call.

The turn card is a 9 of hearts. It misses my hand again.

Wall Street master of the universe hesitates for a moment and then confirms what I already knew.

"I'll check," he says. And he takes a long pull on the last sip of his Jack and Coke. It's a clear concession; he's finishing his drink and going home. He's giving up. If I make any bet here, any bet at all, I'll take down the pot and cap a dominating night. But it's not everything; it's not enough.

"I'll check, too." I tap the table twice with a resigned look on my face.

The river card is the 3 of clubs. I've missed everything. I have 6 high; I can't even beat a bluff, but that shouldn't matter—I can still take this one away.

False master of the universe suddenly reignites his passion for the hand. After counting carefully, he sloppily splashes the pot full of chips; when the maze of green and black and red plastic ovals comes to a final rest in the middle of the table, it's a 640 dollar bet. I can't call. I have six high. I can forfeit and take my 1300 dollar win, or I can raise.

"I'll move all in." I'm stoic and assured.

I'm seeking, craving silence here. Any sound of a voice saying call or a chip hitting the table and I'm shattered. I lose—not just the hand but all of my winnings and the money I bought in with. My gas tank is empty. And most importantly it means I was wrong—about the hand, about master of the universe, about everything. But I know I'm right, and I can't just let him have it.

"What did you say, kid?"

It's a good sign—he's incredulous.

"You were playing it slow the whole way, huh? I might have to fold a huge hand here." It's official now—he has less than nothing.

He "Hollywoods" it, as we like to say, for a few more minutes, seemingly to save face in front of the desperate woman who's been sitting behind him all of these hours; maybe she was his wife, maybe she was a concubine. I could hardly tell the difference. I didn't care—even though he hadn't folded his cards yet, the game was over and I knew it—I was right.

"Alright, you can have it if you really want it that bad, man. I don't even care anymore." He tosses his cards in the muck and plants

an awkwardly aggressive kiss on the less than thrilled wife/concubine character.

I don't show my hand. It's not sportsmanship—he just simply didn't matter enough to me to make him feel defeated. Besides, if I lost, I only would have lost money.

John Carrigan skipped a few lines and then wrote towards the bottom of the page:

In the end and when it matters, I am my father's son.
John W. Carrigan.
November 12, 2000.

John sat back on his bed, hand rubbing the back of his now sweaty, entangled hair for a few seconds, and decided to push on through the journal to the second and third tenets.

Sports/Politics—The result of both of these entities is identical, but for different, diametrically opposing reasons. In both, one can lose without consequence, which is the beautiful thing about sports and the infuriating thing about politics—infuriating because people never, anywhere in the world, come to understand it. Sport is beautiful, or can be, because in what other pursuit can you give all of your sweat and opportunity for heartbreak, too, that will cost you nothing at all if you lose? There's a purity in that which is unmatched in the rest of the natural and man-made world alike.

John quickly remembered the day Roger Clemens lost his perfect game in the bottom of the ninth at Fenway Park and the look of devastation on his father's face. That look had always been a harrowing if not tragic memory. It seemed okay now. He read on, almost voraciously now.

Politics are of no consequence because they literally mean nothing, because they are beneath us, because they make us small. There are some things that are true. There are some things that we believe in an interminable way. The concept that people can and should live in a homeland without imperial intrusion and practice their religion without affront or hegemony or external pressure or persuasion are things that are primordially true. But I have come to realize, too late in my life, perhaps, that winning and losing politically on these truths is a wretched kind of nothingness. I live in a homeland. I practice my religion. These things are no less true if they fail to be recognized by a decree. They are no less true even when an Oliver Cromwell plows through our countryside and exterminates us. Thoreau and Emerson had these tenets exactly right—we rise through bad policy so why do we think that good policy has any efficacy? It is so simple. It is so startling, I am ashamed that it took me so long to understand something so natural, something so embedded in us. I am deeply sorry for all those who have died. I am deeply sorry for any of those who have lost a moment's sleep pondering such questions.

John stopped reading. The self-flagellation and attempts at reconciliation went on for a few more pages, but John had read all he needed to read. He understood. The cause of his father's death had quickly become even more shrouded and confusing, but it also became wholly immaterial. As he skipped through to find the next section, an arcane piece of parchment folded in thirds fell out of the notebook. It was a copy of the 1916 Easter Proclamation published in the *Irish Daily News.* It had blood on it. It was faded and crusted, but it was blood. It was a deep, auburn stain on the top right corner and smears of it obscured some of the sentences in the middle few paragraphs. John had read the proclamation half a dozen times before. He decided to read it again now.

In the name of God and of the dead generation from which she receives her nationhood, Ireland, through us, summons her children to her flag and strikes for her freedom...

We declare the right of the people of Ireland to the ownership of Ireland, and to the unfettered conrol of Irish destinies, to be sovereign and indefeasible. The long usurpation of that right by foreign people and government has not extinguished that right, nor can it ever be extingished but by the destruction of the Irish people...Standing on that funadamental right and again asserting it at arms in the face of the word, we hereby proclaim the Irish Republic as a Sovereign Independent State, and we pledge our lives and the lives of our comrades-in-arms to the cause of its freedom, of its welfare, and of its exaltation among the nations.

The Irish Repubic is entitled to and hereby claims the allegiance of every Irishman and Irishwoman. The Republic guarantees religious and civil liberty, equal rights and equal opportunities to all its citizens, and declares its resolve to pursue the happiness and prosperity of the whole nation and all of its parts, cherishing all the children of the nation equally, and oblivious to the differences carefully fostered by an alien government, which have divided a minority and majority in the past…

We place the cause of the Irish Republic under the cause of the Most High God. Whose blessing we invoke upon our arms, and we pray that no one who serves that cause will dishonour it by cowardice, inhumanity ,and rapine. In this supreme hour the Irish nation must, by its valour and its discipline and by the readiness of its children to sacrifice themselves for the common good, prove itself worthy of the august destiny to which it is called.

John Carrigan had read the Proclamation of the Irish Republic half a dozen times or so before, but this was the first time he paused to think about it. He picked up his pen again:

I am my father's son. I am in Irishman. It is a settled cause unable to be disturbed or affirmed.
John W. Carrigan.
Novemenber 12, 2000.

John scrolled down the parchment and looked at the signatures, all names that appeared and disappeared in shadows in Irish folklore. There was also a homemade signature ink. It was faint, but perceptible—*Kiernan John Carrigan.*

So that was it; for all the fanfare and all the requiem set to guitar and scribbled in ink about the indominable Kiernan Carrigan, Kiernan and John's father were just two people who were supposed to be dead. John decided that they both seemed okay with it, and suddenly he seemed okay with it. But he hoped, quite fervently for the first time that he could remember, that he would be a Dr. Agnes Vladnowitz. Being a person who was supposed to be dead seemed okay for his father, and even for the mystical Kiernan Carrigan, but it wasn't good enough for John. He shivered, wondering what he could do to stop the tide, but he quickly gathered some resoluteness and kept pushing through the journal until he found the section on the final tenet. It was the shortest section, the shortest by a good deal.

> *Love without requital—Don't shun requital for the sake of shunning, but don't discredit the love you feel if it doesn't stay, or if you can't stay. Love is love and it is the single best thing we do, precisely because we don't do it, we just feel it and it exists with its own inertia. That is never inviolate simply because it doesn't remain or "work out" or because we don't occupy its physical space anymore. That kind of thinking is the most profane kind of results-oriented philosophy. Love is not a result of other things.*

That was it—that was how the section, and the entire journal ended, abruptly and without digression. John briefly wondered if his parents marriage was requited, if marriage itself was a kind of indefatigable requital, but he didn't trouble himself too much with it. It was love it seemed, and that was something. He did wonder if his mother felt the same.

He fell asleep, clothes and shoes on, one of the laces of the left shoe of his pair of Adidas Superstars—the white shell-tops with the three black stripes—dangling over his foot and being caressed by the cold autumn breeze rushing in through the opened bedroom window.

NOVEMBER 13, 2000

Carrigan awoke refreshed but disoriented; there were no clocks left in his old bedroom. He opened the blinds quickly, almost covetous of what new landscape might appear. It was bright. It was morning. He walked to the kitchen to look for his mother. All throughout his childhood Carrigan could find his mother at the kitchen table in the morning, no matter when he rose from bed. He wondered if she heard him creeping and rushed out to be there, or just had some divine instinct that allowed her to rise moments before him and post up in the kitchen—a relaxed, serene figure of constancy and thoughtfulness and ease. She was there again today, ostensibly reading a newspaper, her eyes bright, prepared to hear any myriad of news—whether it be regarding a last second basket in a school game, or the death of her husband.

Carrigan finally found a clock as he sat across from his mother; it was 9:29 am.

"What time did I head up to the room?"

"7."

"PM?"

"Yes, John. Class today?"

"No, nothing on Fridays since second term freshman year."

"What are you going to do today?

"Hold on," Carrigan said as he rubbed his eyes open and started to gain some footing and become aware of his surroundings. "You're really not curious?"

"About what, John?"

"Come on."

"I said you could tell me what you liked. I meant it. You're not the kind of person who needs to be reminded of things you want to do."

"Okay, well, tell me something about him Mom. Anything you like."

"Well, the truth is most of the activities were secrets to me, too. I will absolutely tell you about any events that I'm aware of. That's your right if you want to know, though I honestly can't think of any good it could do, or how it could really matter—the old things are not the new things, and the ones that are, are the last things you should think about anyway."

Emily Carrigan wasn't hostile, but seemed almost resigned, and for the first time John could remember, she seemed to be grasping; anxiously trying to piece together a coherent narrative of a career that it was all too clear she knew as little about as her son. She hesitated a good deal, as one tends to do when faced with the the conflict of feeling morally obligated to do something one didn't want to do, or, more accurately, when facing a task one found herself completely unequipped to perform.

"The year before you were born, he signed a letter to a newspaper—"

"Stop, Mom, no," John interrupted. "I don't mean biographical things. I couldn't care less about that. I meant, what was he like to be around?"

John's mother leaned back with eyes closed and smiled wryly. She breathed deeply and audibly in and out, and it became apparent she hadn't really been breathing up to this point in the conversation.

"You don't remember anything, John?"

"Sure, I remember some things, but I was little. What was he like to be around, you know, as another adult and all?"

"Charming."

"I'm sure, Mom."

"He was never angry or frustrated or bitter or short or dismissive when he was talking to you, when you were in the room with him."

John smiled; it was nice to hear that his father was personable, and that he had presence. But it was painfully obvious that the qualifying clause in his mother's response implied that his father was far too often stricken with all of those harrowing and unattractive emotions otherwise, and they seemed to fuel much of the shame he was apologizing for in the political section of his journalistic treatise.

"What did he like?"

"He loved cultural art John—movies, music. If we went to the movies, I'd have to beg him to let me sleep afterwards; he'd want to dissect every scene with me, talk about every acting choice and every possible implication."

"Things you put your whole heart into that had no consequence," John murmered softly.

"What?"

"Nothing. I'm sorry, Mom. Go on."

But she didn't go on, at least not right away. She stopped abruptly, and her left hand impulsively covered her soft mouth. John was sure she was remembering one of those conversations about film that she had feigned sleep during and turned away from, and realizing now that she'd never get to feign sleep again, never get the luxury of waiting until tomorrow to hear something her husband said.

John instantly recalled that opening day Little League home-run that he had hit right after returning to America after his father's death. He remembered his mother standing by herself in the bleachers amongst the throngs of suburban, mundane couples with their folding chairs and white socks pulled up past their shins and subtle paunches hanging over the waistlines of shorts that were a bit too short or jeans that had been worn for a few years too many. Emily Carrigan was stylistic and worldly and reserved, but was very much alone. Some of her fellow revellers were parents, some were step-parents, and even many grandparents, and aunts and uncles with too much time on their hands and too little stimulation in their own lives, but all were arranged in couples.

John ached for his mother again—ached for her more deeply than he had since that day of adolescent baseball glory, and more profoundly this time, because he felt like he understood. He felt like talking now, but he would never ask her why she didn't remarry—why she never even seemed to consider it. It seemed profane to be open about things so deeply rooted and tucked away in one's psyche, although people seemed to go on television to do just that. People forefeited their mystery for empathy or a canned sense of absolution, or worse, just so people would look at them, and it was just profane. Carrigan was proud of his mother for guarding hers so deeply, so resolutely, so powerfully that no one even seemed to consider asking her personal questions.

The interval in their conversation continued as both flipped through different sections of the newspaper, sipping beverages—John orange juice, his mother, tea—in silent agreement that the abrupt hiatus in their conversation would be ignored and not treated as awkward or in need of further inquiry, as both retreated to the recesses of the mind for contemplation and speculation. They understood each other. After five full minutes, John waded back in, without warning or preface or apology, which was new for him.

"What was his favorite movie?"

"Well his favorite Irish movie was—"

"*The Quiet Man,*" John interrupted.

"He told you? Oh, there was something about it in that journal? I can't say I'm surpised."

"Nope. Neither."

"Then how?"

"Mom, how could it not be? Little Mikaline Flynn. John Wayne dragging Maureen O'Hara all over the Burren out there in County Clare."

"Your father liked it for other reasons."

"Such as?"

"An Ireland of all landscape and no politics."

"I get it."

"And a love story that ended with the wedding."

"I'll leave that alone, I suppose."

"Your father had some quirks." She ran her hand threw the midnight black hair bespeckled with vibrant gray.

"Did he have a favorite non-Irish movie?"

"*Butch Cassidy and the Sundance Kid.*"

"The appeal of escape," John said whimsically.

"I prefer the appeal of companionship," his mother responded quickly and fervently.

"Well I suppose escaping with a companion is about the best you can hope to do," John said with tenderness in his voice as he leaned in and pattted the back of his mother's wrist.

"He was a romantic John—a lifestyle romantic."

"What does that mean?"

"He was enthralled by the ambience of things—the old world. Sealing envelopes, and riding on train cars bound for cities that had pasts, and subterfuges in hotel lobbies, peering out over opened newspapers and staring intently at duplicitous, conspiratorial bellhops, and anecdotal, personal stories about iconic figures who people only knew from stories in university lecture halls, and the importance of song lyrics, and the beauty of individual sentences in novels no one ever read.

And he loved the Red Sox because they came back to Boston every April regardless of how wretched the previous Septemeber or October turned out. I tried to tell him that it was their job and that all of the other teams came back every April, too, but he never wanted to hear that. He was your kind of guy, John. You would've really liked him."

Both Emily Carrigan and her son smiled, but the word "would've" had a visible effect on both of them, and not merely for the obvious implication of lost time and experience, but for the very clear inference that he didn't like him in his remembered form or hollogram. John sniffled agressively and returned to the veil of his orange juice glass.

"Well, it's just a shame he had to die in the 1980's of all decades," John said with sardonic levity in his voice.

"Why do you say that?'

"He was a culture guy, and the 80's are just as bad as it gets. The music, the movies—I mean, come on."

"You're such a snob. I love you John, but you really are."

"Who does that reflect on?'

"The university."

"It's not my fault I came of age in an atmosphere of cultural genius known as the 1990's."

"Well, those are over now too," Emily said austerely. "Maybe you'll feel differently about them in ten years. Though I sort of hope you don't."

She left the kitchen, almost automatically, patting her son John, her fourth child of seven in all, five still living, on the shoulder, and exited without saying why she was leaving or where she was going, but anyone who didn't know her would've thought she was off to the last soccer match of a prep school autumn.

John walked to the phone and dialed impulsively. A familiar voice picked up.

"Jane? It's John—I'm not really sure if I get to say 'it's me' at this point, or what the protocol for something like that is, so I'll just go with 'hi Jane, its John.'"

"The fact that you spoke three full sentences before I even got to say hello properly gave away the fact that it was you."

"It was actually one sentence, with a bunch of dashes and commas and such."

"What's up, John?"

"Are you still doing intersession in Dublin?"

"Yep. Trinity College. Why?"

"If I said I wanted to come too?"

She hesitated, searching for pathos, or just searching for stridency.

"I don't think you need my permission."

"But would you want me to come?"

"I don't think you get to ask me that yet."

John paused and tried to interpret playfulness or flirtation in her voice. He couldn't count on it. After a moment, he said, "Richie Randall is going too."

"Is that the kid who got his pancreas removed?"

"No, you're thinking of someone else. I don't even think you can get your pancreas removed."

"You can get anything removed, John."

"Well, anyway, I just called to let you know that I was coming—wanted to be up front and all."

"That's so intoxicatingly noble of you, John. I'll talk to you soon, okay?"

"Yeah, okay."

She was still calling him John, not Carrigan.

"One last thing," John desperately exclaimed before she could go.

"Yes?"

"Do you want to take a boat instead of a plane?"

"No, no I do not."

Jane hung up first. She yielded him no favor, no grace, no hint of what she was feeling. He craved her with an intensity that he never felt before.

John followed the sound of the television into the living room and found his mother.

"Mom, so there's this six week intersession course at Trinity that I think I'm going to do."

"Oh."

"My friend Richie Randall is going, too."

"Is he that kid who has three girlfriends all named Melissa?" she said casually as she flipped through the channels, landing on a documentary about the Kennedy assasination.

"No, you're thinking of someone else."

"I see."

"Jane is going too."

"I see—interesting that you didn't mention that first."

"Well, I just didn't."

"You'll miss Christmas."

"I won't miss Christmas. I'll miss this Christmas."

"Alright then, John."

DECEMBER 21, 2000

The Penguin edition of *Portrait of the Artist as a Young Man,* the one featuring Joyce with hands plunged into cordoroy pockets and a fresh white cap on his head on the cover, always faced outward from Carrigan's bookshelf. The self-satisfied, taciturn, borderline smug look on Joyce's freshly shaven face was a taunting kind of challenge that Carrigan preferred to keep ever present. It was a challenge from a man who knew what his accomplishments were, and from a man who just seemed agonizingly more Irish than he was; so indellibly Irish, in fact, that even after engendering his own exile in a whim of disgust, had become the subject of nearly divine iconography in his home city. The city of Dublin.

Joyce had run away to Paris, and he had initially mortified Dubliners to the point of venom with his portrayals in *Ulysses,* and still they came to worship him, and still it seemed he failed to care, and there was a kind of honesty in that that seemed quite foreign to the point of being counter to the truth of human vanity and frailty. A man so brazen yet so humble in his commitment to his craft. A man who achieved reverence by reviling its pursuit, and who now stood everywhere, imortally everywhere, in the city of Dublin in bronze and marble statued salute, adorned with a cane that spoke dignity and not weariness, and an austerity untouched by the rain and unbroken by the change of everything else.

Today, as Carrigan waited at Gate 42 of Boston's Logan Airport, he held that Penguin edition of *Portrait* clutched in his left hand, as if the two of them would return to Dublin together, a kind of dual repatriation of sorts in which one of them had been forgiven all of his sins, and the other was still unsure of what his sins were. But John Carrigan was the last Carrigan born in Dublin, and that connected him to something. It had a touch of the ethereal in it, and anyway, it was good to have an extra set of eyes, no matter how smug, no matter how impossible.

Richard Peter Randall, Richie since birth, found Gate 42 right as Carrigan was placing his Joyce edition back into his over-the-shoulder bag. Carrigan and Richie had been friends since meeting in the first grade, though to Carrigan, friendship was exactly what he had told Jane it was—an implied bond based on memory and feeling—not an obligation to maintain physical proximity or even semi-frequent correspondence. It didn't mean any less to him though, and that's what he so struggled to convince others of; Richie didn't seem to mind, or maybe he minded so much that he decided to come on this impromtu odyssey to Dublin despite the fact that he had already been there (with a band that was semi-successful, and that Richie had quit at the exact moment that it had grown repetitive) and didn't particularly care for (he had brought a basketball with him and didn't find a hoop in the entire city to shoot it in; Carrigan had encountered a similar problem when he had been there) .

Richie didn't go to Yale, and in fact, he didn't go to any college for that matter. He had to register for spring classes at a local community college just to officially have a "home university" and be qualified to enroll in Trinity's study abroad session. Carrigan was absolutely positive that come the end of January some hopeful young adjunct professor at Gateway Community College would receive no reply as he repeated "Richard Randall" during commencing roll call, but he didn't bring it up; he liked Richie too much to articulate what they both already knew—that Richie had become a pretend college student and agreed to fly across the Atlantic simply to spend some time with a friend that he missed quite dearly. He didn't bring it up because Richie never would; he never sought love or deference. He was funny without affect or effort or want. He was fashionable but not hip or self-concerning. He was the only American Carrigan ever knew who loved Marley but didn't smoke weed (he also loved early Stones, late Mozart, and the Wu-Tang Clan, in that order). He performed famously with women, in that they would be laughing with him within ten minutes after catching him kisssing their roommates, friends, or even sisters—he was an impossible boy to stay mad it, even as he came late to everything (he and Carrigan had gone to see the film *Jerry Maguire* as sophomores in high school and Richie found his seat *after* Cuba Gooding had already yelled "Show me the money" two dozen times), and even in the hardening edges of manhood, he remained impossssible to stay mad at, even in the more judgmental and short-tempered efficiency and seriousness and discernible ambition of adulthood he was impossible to feel anything but joy for. He was a deep thinker but never serious. He was the best person Carrigan ever knew, and Carrigan would never purposefully bring a moment of scorn or discomfort to him because he was lucky to call him a friend, and covetous that he would always remain one, even as Carrigan made no renewed or motivated effort to see him more often or call more frequently. It was better this way—better that it come without the ratification of time spent or hours served, better that it come by accident or, at worst, veiled plan or removed third party circumstance.

"I like Ireland because I can wear these elbow patched blazers (he was wearing one for the plane ride) and even put the collar up in the rain and no one thinks I'm pretentious."

He meant it. He wasn't just inventing an excuse to circumvent why he was actually coming.

"No, they still think you're pretentious," said Carrigan.

"Oh."

"Yeah, it's just slightly less obnoxious than wearing one in Cairo or Buenos Aires or Miami, God forbid."

"Well that's exactly what I hated about South America. It was either wear a t-shirt or sweat myself into shock."

Richie had started a Che Guevara inspired *Motorcycle Diaries*-esque tangent across South America the previous summer but quit after Peru simply because he wasn't enjoying himself. He never lied to anyone about aborting the journey before completion—didn't renounce or endorse Che, didn't claim epiphany or revelation or broken-heartedness; he just wasn't having any fun so he hitched a ride to the airport in Lima after a hearty six course meal at one of the city's new haute-cuisine bistros, came back to New Haven, and scored 38 points in a public league basketball game the next afternoon. The day after that he got back on a plane (he hated American summer), landing in Edinburgh to visit a girl he met when he was in the band, and the day after that he travelled into the wild of the Highlands, that were once ruled by the clans and were now owned almost entirely by wealthy internationals, and accompanied her father and brother on the hunt and kill of a red stag outside a familial 17th century lodge. They washed his face in the blood of its innards. It was ritual, they said. His first time. They laughed while they did it. They chanted old Scottish songs on the hike back down, romanticizing the adjacent quarry all the way. Richie vowed never to return to a place where they could exhibit such fierce and raw brutality of spirit and surety but fail to pass even a symbolic independence referendum. The dichotomy was less than manly, he thought. The next day he was back in New York, took the Metro-North train back to New Haven, and scored 34 points in a public league basketball game that evening. Carrigan hoped he would be less restless this summer. He missed his friend.

Richie was drinking a Coke from a glass bottle; he was nothing if not classic, and as he craned the neck of the bottle to squeeze the last fluid ounce out, Carrigan recalled an anecdote involving both of them from right before his father died, or that is to say, right before his father left for Ireland for the last time, and then subsequently died.

Carrigan was in the backseat of the car (a grey Toyota Camry; the only car his father had ever owned) heading to a basketball game, his mother driving and his father in the passenger seat. Richie and his parents were following in the car behind. Peter Carrigan had a garbage bag full of empty bottles and cans with him in the front seat, and every ninety seconds or so, he would drop one out of the window. And every ninety seconds or so, Richie's mother Allison, who had petitioned the local government for recycling ordinances that a dramatic observer might deem Draconian, would screech her car to a halt, pull over, and pick it up. After the third bottle, Emily Carrigan pleaded with her husband to stop, but she laughed while she implored, and Peter Carrigan brushed the hair out of her face and started throwing a bottle or can every minute, and then every thirty seconds or so, and Richie's mother screeched her tires to an immediate halt every time. It was more than a dozen bottles by the time they reached the gym.

"I suppose you think recycling is silly," Allison Randall bellowed as she flung her door open and charged toward the Carrigan's car. I don't know what they do in Ireland, and wherever the hell you run off to disappear, but it's the law here."

All parties looked embarrassed at that last, needlessly personal remark. After all, it would only hurt Carrigan's mother more than his father, anyway.

Peter Carrigan, however, was unfazed. "If I didn't care about recycling, I would've thrown them out the window when you weren't looking. Besides, just be happy this wasn't an away game; I have three more bags in the trunk."

Richie and his father both laughed. Allison Randall turned her back wordlessly and went quickly into the gym, finding an extreme corner seat and affixing herself to it to make sure no one could sit beside her. Richie's parents divorced the next year. Carrigan remembered them arriving separately to the small, informal American wake his mother held for his father the evening before departing for Dublin. Some families live pretty innocuously, he thought, though he didn't really understand it in those terms at that time.

"Where's Jane?" Richie asked upon finishing his Coke.

"I don't know."

Richie paused; he thought that was a suitable retort, and conveyed the incredulity he was feeling most accurately.

"I really don't know."

"I didn't say a word."

"She's on this flight?"

"I believe so."

More silent incredulity was interrupted by the sight of Jane strolling down the corridor, ambling (it was the only appropriate word) leisurely towards the gate. She was actually quite late; they had just made the pre-boarding announcement, but she walked with the austere confidence of a woman who knew they wouldn't leave without her. It wasn't that the flight wouldn't depart; Jane was never so haughty as to believe she had a societal place that would delay airplanes, nor did she ever want one, but more importantly, she knew that the two blokes silently arguing about her at Gate 42 could never leave without her; knew that Carrigan had only come for her, and Richie had only come for Carrigan.

She wore faded blue jeans and a plain grey washed-in sweater, and the weight of the carry-on bag on her left shoulder tugged her sweater upwards at the waist and exposed her pale and toned stomach. The shock of hair that had fallen into her face without being removed that first day she left Carrigan did so again, and again, just as on that day that Carrigan edictally remembered every instance of, Jane made no effort to brush it away. She seemed to understand that important days demanded idiosyncratic nuances to mark them.

"Are you guys ready to go? Come on, they're boarding, and you're just sitting there."

Neither one of them said a word. They just stood up, grabbed their bags, found their boarding passes and their passports, and shuffled off into the forming line at Gate 42.

Richie sat in between them on the plane; he wasn't jealous or feeling left out—it was just the kind of opportunity for a needle he could never let go by. Both Jane and Carrigan respected him for it.

Carrigan rummaged through his bag, and pushing his Joyce edition out of the way, found a volume on Sir Walter Raleigh. As he held it in his lap, he looked through his rain-smeared, blurry window and saw the baggage handlers in their customary red jackets mimicking Michael Jordan fade-aways as they tossed some of the lighter checked luggage into the baggage hold. Carrigan thought again of the absurdity that is the enterprise of flying, and how the seeming whole of man has come to take it so nonchalantly—an abject absurdity becoming commonplace.

Jane leaned over Richie and grabbed the text out of Carrigan's hands.

"Sir Walter Raleigh?"

"Yes. May I have it back now? Snatching is usually considered rude."

It was the first words they had spoken to each other since Carrigan had called to tell her he was coming, her admonition to both he and Richie minutes before notwithstanding. Richie put his headphones on; this exchange clearly wasn't meant for him and he was never the intrusive type.

"You like Sir Walter Raleigh'?" Jane inquired.

"I revere him. Poet, explorer, courtier, imprisoned in the tower on multiple occasions, secret marriage to the Queen's favorite—courtly propriety be damned. He's everything I aspire to be. He's a rogue."

"A rogue," she spit the word out with full-throated disdain. "They don't have The Tower anymore, John. You're not going to end up there during this trip; regardless of how 'rogue-ish' you behave."

Carrigan grit his teeth—she knew him too well. He wondered if he could actually be with someone who knew him that well. He got away with nothing. He never got to pose. He never got to lie—all things essential to his personality. But, even as he pondered these dilemmas, he was fully aware that he was as deeply in love with her as he had ever been.

She went on. "And most of all, John (he hadn't yet decided if the 'John' was similar to the austere formality that accompanied the day she first left him, or if she had just decided that she would start calling him John now; if this was a new stage altogether), he was wretched to the Irish. I mean, how can you miss that? The seizure of lands. The squashing of righteous rebellions. The aristocratic attempts at patronage and peerage. Sir Walter Raleigh? You're kidding me with this. I almost want to get off the plane."

Carrigan wondered if her last sentence was a tacit admission that he was the reason she was coming, but then he remembered that she was scheduled to go on this trip well before he was, and a wave of almost consuming sadness came over him, but only briefly; he was enjoying himself, after all. She dumped the text back in his lap with a rejoicing and arrogant snort of her porcelain nose.

"He's forgiven, Jane."

"Forgiven?"

"And not just in the 'I'm Catholic, so I'm canonically obligated to forgive' fashion either. He disobeyed a monarch for the purpose of love; he tried to overthrow another, and he was executed by an English monarch for political expedience—that's enough expiation for Irish sin for me. (He meant it; he wasn't just making speeches—a point often in need of clarity when it came to Carrigan). He's one of us."

The plane stopped taxiing and the engines roared to intense decibels as Jane opened her mouth (the same customary shock of hair still obscuring its right corner) to respond. John stopped her with a raised hand—"I can't hear you." He made a quick sign of the cross and then put his right hand instinctually on Richie's left shoulder and gripped fairly hard, while closing his eyes, and holding his head suspended just above his knees. Flying—the absurdity of it. Jane looked eagerly past Carrigan and out of his window as the plane ascended sharply, and then fell fully back into her own seat as the plane approached cruising altitude, laying her head back into an almost fully supine position, as her smooth, blush red face became dominated by an enveloping smile. She pushed the notorious shock of hair out of her mouth now, so as to not impede her show of joy in any way. Anyone would have said that she looked content and calm, as if she was waiting for a tide to come cool her feet on some indistinct beach unmarred by the threat of weather or an unwelcomed visitor. And she was not in a rush for the cooling tide to arrive.

The idea that Sir Walter Raleigh was "one of us" demands some qualification. Jane Kiley was from Washington, D.C. She was from Washington because her father was Ireland's ambassador to the United States, and had worked at the Irish embassy in some capacity or another for the entirety of Jane's life. Jane had a far better grasp than Carrigan of what it meant to be Irish and live in the United States. In fairness, she had the advantage of having never lived anywhere else, and in fact, she had only even visited Ireland once—on a three-day sojourn to bury her grandmother out in Inishmore, the largest of the Aran Islands, where the Kiley's had a bit of an ancestral burial ground. She was eight years old then, and all she claimed to remember was the wind blowing the hair into everyone's faces so she couldn't tell who was sad and who was bored and who was looking out to see if the ferry was coming back. It was an inconvenience really, this beautiful place, at least when it was utilized for a morbid or ceremonial purpose. The ferry only returned every three hours or so, and it surely made no exceptions for death. How could it? Ireland has so much of it. And after the wobbly ferry made it back across to Galway or somewhere in County Clare, there was, for most of them, a train or bus ride back to indiscriminate village towns, and then, again for most of them, a 30-40 minute walk back to a cold boarding house or apartment. So one really couldn't blame anyone for keeping a lookout for an approaching ferry and waving on the priest to quicken the pace of his requiem, when he saw that utilitarian ship come boring through the fog of Galway Bay.

Ambassador Declan Kiley was a faithful diplomat and he kept his daughter, his only child (his wife Bridget had experienced near fatal eclampsia giving birth to Jane; there could be no more children), out of Ireland on purpose—he was committed to his work in America and so he wanted his daughter to feel like she was living in a homeland, and not migrating nomadically, out of some sense of staid or official decorum, between two places that she felt slightly alienated from. On this score, he was a raving success; Jane never felt alienated from anywhere.

Declan Kiley looked like an ambassador should look, or that is to say, he looked like how diplomats were portrayed on film—broad shouldered, stone grey hair (it had fully turned that distinguished hue by age 35), barrel-chested without being even slightly intimidating, well-dressed (not in business attire but in the fashionable academic colors of the pubs in the countryside; he looked like a handsome bar extra in one of the opening scenes of *The Quiet Man)*. And he was charmingly loud. He loved Ireland and was no politician; he was meant for the Foreign Service; he wasn't bold enough to be a rebel, but he was too emotional not to care.

The first summer Carrigan and Jane had known each other, she helped him get a summer internship writing speeches for a U.S. senator; they had a habit of inventing excuses to be near each other, and they developed a veritable Tesla versus Edison type rivalry (the inventing kind) when it came to who could most audaciously ask for a date without ever displaying deference or desire. It was as if just asking one another to visit for the summer signified a relinquishing of competitive and amorous hostilities that neither party was ever fully ready for. The next step was just "coupledom" and that seemed onerous to both. It brought normalcy and it brought the beginning of the end of things that felt shocking and terrifying and right. So there was always the sly, diverting requests—the "I have an extra ticket for the game" rejoinders in the place of supplicating inquiries, and to this knowing pageant of subterfuge they were borderline obsequious. This was the first seminal request, however; college wasn't enough—she wanted to see him for the summer and not be interrupted by classes, or shield herself in the slightest with the inoculating and commonplace excuses for absence, like study or sleep. She was his. She was available and she wasn't pretending otherwise.

So on June 1, 1998, Carrigan hitched a ride from his mother over to Union Station in New Haven, bound for Union Station in Washington and something that felt like romance.

"You remember the last time you were in D.C., John?"

"I do."

"Better luck this time."

"They have machines that correct your spelling now, anyway."

As the train migrated south and the cities whirled past, cities with names but no faces—cities like Newark, Trenton, Philadelphia, and Wilmington—all hamlets to which he had never been, Carrigan's calm dissipated in lock step with each new halt of the train, and by Baltimore, he had grown downright fidgety. When the train finally reached Union Station in Washington, he made up his mind once and for all that five hours was the maximum he could spend on any continuous travel excursion, whatever the cause and regardless of the destination. He walked directly through the front foyer and out the front door; the Capital Building, his new, temporary place of employment (all capital employment is transient, he supposed), peered at him from directly across the street, and cast a domineering shadow over the liminal D.C. skyline. He paused for no more than fifteen seconds to look at it, and then hung a sharp right and descended the Metro escalator, finding a red line train towards Dupont Circle, and the opulent sanctuary that was Massachusetts Avenue and Embassy Row, and the quasi-Irish soil that lay inside the veneer of the brick and mortar of the Kiley residence. It represented the totality of being Irish and living in America; feeling partially exposed as a fraud to each place, not a self-loathsome fraud per se, but a small yet constant tinge of both superficiality and superciliousness gnawing somewhere in the recesses of the consciousness. Carrigan thought of his last trip to Dublin—pointing at menus whenever possible to mask the absence of his brogue.

Jane and her father were waiting for Carrigan outside of the gate of the embassy. Jane's hands were buried in the pockets of her faded-in jeans, and she was bobbing her left heel up and down; she actually seemed nervous, and Carrigan immediately felt relaxed. She wore a yellow tank top that exposed the lovely browning skin on her shapely shoulders and the full nape of her languorous neck. Declan Kiley was 5'11, a good three inches smaller than Carrigan, but Carrigan always felt like a small boy when he was around him. It wasn't just the effect of mere raw physicality or strength of shoulders (Carrigan's were quite slight); it was that he always kept his gaze fixed, a kind of melancholy, close-mouthed, half smile gaze, on Carrigan, even when a third party, even when his daughter, was the one talking. John Carrigan suspected that Ambassador Declan Kiley knew exactly how his father had died.

"Jane tells me you're a Philosophy major, lad."

"Well I do take some Philosophy, sir."

"Do you know Marcus Aurelius?"

"Some."

"I favor Book Eight of *Meditations.* 'Regret is a censure of yourself for missing something beneficial. The good must be something beneficial, and of concern to the wholly good person. No wholly good person would regret missing a pleasure. Therefore pleasure is neither beneficial nor a good.'"

He had found a clever way to dissuade Carrigan from having sex with his daughter. He had clearly planned it for a while; he was not the type of man with Marcus Aurelius on the tongue. He was very proud of himself. Jane and Carrigan both laughed; he deserved the good cheer.

Carrigan had a room in the American University dorms over in Tenleytown, which was also off the red line. He was two days earlier than the rest of his summer study cohort. Jane said goodbye to her father, who waved heartily at both of them, and walked into the Dupont Circle metro with Carrigan. The Shady Grove train arrived just as they were reaching the platform. They laughed off Marcus Aurelius within an hour later; Jane's yellow tank top sparking a flint of color on the linoleum floor—her faded-in jeans covering his khaki pants with the cuffs rolled, over the back of the otherwise bare desk chair. Jane was brilliant; relaxed yet intense and she moved like rhythm. She smelled like a woman. She lacked all self-consciousness. She was in love. Carrigan didn't know if she had had practice, or if she was just one of those people born to be good at this sort of thing. He didn't ask. Either way, she seemed the doyenne of her generation, and Carrigan was sure of it, even while lacking any means of comparison. It was this memory, this purely corporeal image that was the last half conscious, half waking thought he had before the pilot announced their final descent into Dublin, and Carrigan looked out of his now translucently clear window at that different kind of green, for the third time in his life, or at least the third time he was aware of.

DECEMBER 24-25, 2000

The three days prior to Christmas Eve had been largely organizational—the unpacking of bags, the reading of texts that had gone ignored, and the psychological immersion in the anachronistic and entirely seductive echo chamber that is Trinity College Dublin. It was to be a 15-day intersession, and the only days the college took off were Christmas, and New Year's Day. Richie was enthralled by Trinity from the start and took to sitting in the Long Room library for hours on end. He would've gladly slept there each night, but at around 5:00 pm each afternoon (they called the closing hour "dusk," despite the fact that it was an indoor facility), a security guard wearing a blue blazer and responding to mumbled commands on a walkie-talkie gently tapped him on the shoulder, often waking him out of a semi-conscious slumber, and told him it was to time to head back to the dorms; the Long Room was really more of a museum now—even the stacks were roped off and were only accessible by a ladder that was never present. But there was still that unmistakable aroma—that stale paper mustiness that only a true man of letters can ever really enjoy. It was a kind of shibboleth for those who fancied themselves men of letters, to sit there in that room without disdain or headache or nausea, and Richie was passing the test. It wasn't a conversion for him; he had always been a man of letters, decree or otherwise. He was a humble parish priest visiting St. Peter's Basilica for the maiden time. When he stood up to depart each day, the waning quarter light from the high above panes always burned his eyes into a squint, and he immediately felt hungry and restless, while feeling no regret.

Jane was registered for four intensive classes; she had suffered from a bought of disenchantment back home (what a strange phrase that suddenly seemed) and taken only one class in the fall. And while her academic disenchantment (she couldn't quite articulate why she felt the way she did; she enjoyed the acting class and performed famously—it was really more of a malaise brought on by the knowledge that ordinary people were also doing it without fanfare or enlightenment or emotional breakdown) had not yet subsided, she had decided to continue it, if it should continue into the following fall—she was never wedded to the continuation of a state of mind; her father claimed to enjoy Marcus Aurelius but she was much more of an Emersonian—with degree in hand, lest it become an excuse for the absence of experience or an all frills job in public affairs at the embassy in Dupont. So she spent her days in class, and her nights reading for class, but walked down Grafton into the park with Carrigan after dinner each day.

They watched the ducks and swans in the gloaming from the gazebo located about 150 yards to the left of the north entrance. They often didn't talk at all; it was an enhancement of any intimacy they had shared before. The ducks were unseemly but kind to the young visitors who wished to throw them bread, or even stale donuts. The swans were majestic and clean and the untrained were always surprised and discombobulated the first time they witnessed their abject bitterness and ferocity. The high school metaphor was too apt, and so neither Jane nor Carrigan offered it. Besides, they enjoyed not talking.

There came a time in each of these endeavors— it wasn't after the same amount of repose each day, it was much more random than that, as the revelation was much more natural than it was preordained or carefully considered—that Carrigan became more distant and dour. Jane could notice it immediately even in the absence of speech, or perhaps because of it. And she suspected that she knew the cause; sometimes it affronted him swiftly and in the middle of a sonorous reverie, and sometimes it advanced gradually through him like an omnibus kind of resonant disease—but every day, as he filtered out the twilight with a woman he loved in St. Stephen's Green, there came a time when he became aware that it was highly unlikely that anyone would even think to fire an assassin's bullet at him.

His ancestors, he thought, might be happy at that, might even be relieved or fulfilled, but Carrigan imagined the commentary of such apparitions to be in the similar conceit to that of the painter stricken with madness who tells his son to avoid the artistic life while never wishing to do anything else himself. There was vigor in allegiance to delusion or the abstract. Jane wasn't exactly right on the plane—they still do have The Tower of London; it's just that now anyone with 12 pounds and a sight-seeing map could find his way to the top, snap some photographs and feign intrigue to his restless children, while his bored wife stood apart in the doorway and smiled wanly and thought of Sir Walter Raleigh and became sad in a way that she couldn't quite fathom because she had never desired anything other than exactly the life that she had and that now, suddenly, seemed so disappointing. But here, in Dublin, at the end of the millennial New Year that was identical to all the new years that Jane and Carrigan had ever known, Jane stopped Carrigan before his requiems morphed into wallowing. She would take John's arm when it was time to leave and lead him silently back out onto Grafton. They would stop for ice cream and stand listening to a well-dressed busker play Tracy Chapman's *Fast Car* or something new by David Grey, *Babylon* if it was a big crowd, and the more sanguine *Say Hello, Wave Goodbye* if not. Trinity would be illuminated by the time they returned to the front gate. Showing their badges they would part under the arch in the main rotunda; Jane to her room to read, Carrigan to his room to wait for the next time.

Tonight, the three of them walked up O'Connell together and towards Midnight Mass. A few blocks north of the spire they would turn right onto Marlborough Street and walk around a small bend that took them to the entrance of St. Mary's. They found three seats together, Richie once again in the middle, as the orchestra was playing the processional.

"Are you even Catholic?" Jane asked Richie. She wasn't mad he was there, just genuinely curious.

"I like ritual."

"Really? I'm surprised."

"I like ritual in small, non-abundant doses. Midnight Mass seems perfect."

The answer satisfied all parties. The mass moved along with the proper balance of alacrity and reflection, and Father Holt delivered an eloquent, if not particularly meaningful, homily. After the Lord's Prayer, the offerings of peace commenced. Richie and Jane laughed awkwardly as they gave each other a hardy and aggrandized handshake. Jane then confidently and gracefully stepped through Richie and kissed Carrigan softly on the mouth, lingering the total amount of time one could linger on a kiss in church and not be leered at. Carrigan instinctively held her waist with his left hand. None of them spoke until they found their way back out onto O'Connell following the recessional and Jane announced she was going on ahead to read.

"Merry Christmas."

"Merry Christmas."

"Merry Christmas."

Jane hurried ahead, jaywalking through the dividing intersection. Carrigan and Richie were maybe 50 yards behind.

"It didn't mean anything, Richie."

"She didn't kiss me like that, Carrigan. Go, catch up to her. I want to go meet up with somebody anyway and I'll feel less bad about abandoning you now."

Carrigan hustled past the Liffey, squeezing through throngs standing three shoulders across but still didn't find her, so he slowed down, and instead knocked on the door of her room after a leisurely walk. She answered, leaning against her half-opened door, without any vernal greeting.

"Do you love me again?" Carrigan asked directly and without equivocation even in gesture.

"I wouldn't have come here if I didn't. Now go, I have to read."

Carrigan left without denouement, in fact turning to leave immediately to avoid any impression of one. Upon reaching his room he opened his window to let the frigid December island air in, carried on white bursts of billowing cold. He sat in bed, knees bent up against his chest for a short time and then lay supine under his comforter and commenced a dreamless, restful sleep. Jane fell asleep with an open Pascal volume on her chest laying face up, her arm keeping the book from folding in. She dreamed briefly of the future but mostly of nothing other than melodies she heard buskers play on Grafton Street that afternoon. She would be alive for six more days.

JANUARY 1, 2001

January 1, 2001 was the day that Jane Kiley died. It is vulgar to render death as suspense for the purpose of storytelling; there should be no purposeful build-up, no foreshadowing hints, no notes of blissful contrasting experience from the days between Midnight Mass and the day Jane died, which somehow solely function to make the death seem sadder to strangers. It just comes, and the ceremony afterwards dissipates quickly; people have to catch the next ferry back to Galway, after all.

Jane had read and gone to class in the week prior to her death, and in fact, had even abandoned taking the post-dinner sojourns into the park with Carrigan, as essays were starting to come due. But she agreed to come to Howth today; had agreed to spend the last open schedule day in Ireland climbing into the hills above the Irish Sea. The three of them walked back up O'Connell together, just as they had done on Christmas Eve, but this time took a right directly parallel to the great spire, and walked another mile or so down to the Connolly railway station. They bought day fare tickets for the 25-minute train ride to Howth, the sea becoming more visible with every passing stop. The conductor bellowed "Binn Éadair" as the train stopped for the last time. "That's us," Carrigan said, and they all rose together.

They first curved around the front of the station, walking away from the village and out to the end of the pier at Howth Head where the sea was breaking against ashen rocks and people were taking pictures.

"Come on," Carrigan said, pointing into the hills. "It's crowded here; let's walk up into the cliffs." They all agreed. Richie had picked up a soccer ball that seemed without an owner and he and Jane were kicking it to each other, and then throwing it to each other and calling each other Americans.

The first half of the journey into the cliffs over Howth could be traversed by hiking up a paved road where decadent houses featuring satellite dishes overlooked the sea. There was an unkempt set of stairs descending to the beach about halfway up the road, and the three went slowly down to the shore level, Richie and Carrigan skipping rocks, Jane removing her shoes and rolling up the cuffs of her red pants to linger a while in the frozen water. She didn't shout or brace at the cold; just looked out to sea and found her shoes again as her body started to tremble. Fifteen minutes later they had reached the impasse where the road merges with the uneven slope of the highest cliffs. They were all tired, but kept going, reasoning that the trip back down would seem easier if they descended from the highest point. Logic had no value—there were four more days left in an Ireland they were just beginning to understand and nobody wanted to sit on the train back to campus yet.

Jane ran ahead; she was running ahead in fits and starts since the beach to shake the aquatic cold lingering in her toes. She reached a large flat clump of earth about fifty feet above where Carrigan and Richie lingered behind. The cliffs reached to about 560 feet at their highest level, and Jane was about 150 feet shy of that.

"Throw me the soccer ball. I want to punt it out to sea. It'll take forever to fall down."

Richie obliged and flipped the ball underhanded, looping towards Jane. It was a perfect throw but Jane misread its trajectory. She stepped quickly right and her right foot skidded off the green moss traversing the fracture of the flat, smooth rock, and as she moved to stabilize herself her momentum lurched forward. Finding no stick or catch to any surface up in the wild high cliffs, she was gone. To an observer witnessing the scene only from the end of the episode, it would've looked as if she was literally running off the cliffs and into the sea.

Carrigan and Richie stood frozen in place for a moment, both instinctively not wanting to watch the descent. Carrigan then sprinted to the edge. He saw nothing.

"Jane!"

"Jane!" He screamed only her name. It is a wonder why people scream names in moments of tragedy. It is almost an unwilling and unconscious admonishment—just listen to this instruction and you'll make it out. Just listen and respond and whatever it is that is happening doesn't have to happen; or at least not so quickly, and so without mercy or rehearsal or second chance. Richie joined in calling her name.

Still seeing nothing, Carrigan turned and sprinted back down the hill and onto the paved road. He sprinted all the way down, falling three times, and hurting himself quite badly the second time. His face seared with the burn of the road he had collapsed into. He made it down to shore's level in about five minutes and dove wildly into the bay, discarding only his shoes. Jane's lifeless body had already been brought to the pier by a man in a two-seated wooden vessel. Carrigan climbed out of the bay as Richie reached the bottom of the hill, and they walked together, Richie holding Carrigan up, towards the encircled and silent crowd.

"I'm sorry, lad," said the boater who had fished Jane out with both of his bare hands as an angler might do to do a large game fish on the green wooded shores of the Amazon. His name was Eamon Duffy. He was from Bray and had just sailed over that morning.

"Are you lads Americans?"

Carrigan didn't answer. Richie had already begun walking back towards the train station. Carrigan reached into Jane's soaking left pocket, removed her wallet, and followed closely behind. He never looked at her face.

JANUARY 3, 2001

The only way to make it to Inishmore in time for the service was by way of a tourist bus leaving from upper O'Connell Street at 5:00 am. It would stop in Doolin so the (mostly) Americans could buy fudge from a Swedish ex-pat, and then stop out at the Burren so they could take pictures, and then on to Galway where people could stay on the bus and continue on to the Cliffs of Moher, or ferry over to the Aran Islands. Carrigan was the only one who ferried out to the islands this morning, and he was sure his fellow travelers were glad to be rid of him. It was his second Irish funeral, and this time, he cried the whole way there, stopping only to gather enough breath to start again minutes later. He was stoic and dehydrated by the time he reached the tip of Inishmore. He had packed neither tie nor jacket and was wearing one of Richie's pretentious cobalt blazers with over-sized brown elbow patches. He recognized no one, save Ambassador Declan Kiley; he hadn't met Jane's mother before today.

The Requiem Mass (*Missa Defunctorum)* was said in Latin. Carrigan understood every third or fourth word. When the congregation proceeded out to the burial ground where eight-year-old Jane had been so caught up with the hair blowing into everyone's faces at her grandmother's funeral, all Carrigan could do was look out to sea for the arrival of the ferry. He didn't want or mean to, but it seemed as if everyone was covertly raising their solemn heads every few minutes to gaze into the engrossing fog in search of deliverance from this place. Carrigan could swear his saw Declan Kiley doing it at least once or twice. Later that evening, the director of the Trinity intersession knocked on Carrigan's door to ask if he'd like for them to arrange bereavement airfare tickets for himself and Richie. Carrigan told her they already had tickets; he knew Richie wanted to stay to the finish, and where was there to go anyway? He told the director thank you and wished her a goodnight before she could engage him further. He had turned 22 years old around 12 hours before Jane had died.

JANUARY 6, 2001

Carrigan and Richie sat on the runway of the Dublin Airport, Richie occupying the window seat this time.

"Thanks for agreeing to fly into Washington instead of Boston. I'm happy you came here."

"I missed you, John."

John Carrigan found his way to Embassy Row in Dupont Circle again, and as he waited outside of the gate for Jane's father, alone this time, he kept his gaze focused on the Irish and American flags both flying at half-staff. Declan Kiley came out to Massachusetts Avenue, and the two men shook hands. Declan asked John some questions about the spring term that he couldn't really answer, and John gave the ambassador his daughter's wallet.

"Do you want to know how your father died, lad?"

"No thank you, sir."

And that was that. They shook hands again and Carrigan descended into the Dupont Metro station, feeling sadness without affectation for the first time in his life.

SPRING 2001

The end of the last season of philosophy wasn't a series of events, or even translatable in tales of discernibly discriminate days. It also can't be called anti-climax if, by nature, there is no inherent climax. College was for Carrigan, in the spring of 2001, just as it had always been—a kind of lucidly livable waking dream characterized by the site of overgrown green trees that lined a nondescript, always green campus lawn. The air was always diaphanous and the scene was always the same, save the pitiable detail of which people were walking by that lush nondescript lawn on any given day. That was the joy and the deadening brand of sadness. He realized that he was no longer 21 sometime in February, and that composed in equal parts the joy and the deadening sadness of the season for him. It was all a place that could never end and a place where no one person could ever stay. It was Whitman's "corpse" waiting the proper time in the doorway; its otherwise perfect beauty diminishing in exact proportion to how long one overstayed one's welcome. It had eternity but no repetition. Carrigan joined the baseball team and hit .367. Men don't come of age; they are remnants of certain ages, and there are no sad stories in the tales of deposed kings, but only wearisome sadness in the deposed thoughts of kingship as a mortal entity.

OTHER
ANAPHORA LITERARY
PRESS TITLES

PLJ: Interviews with Gene Ambaum and Corban Addison: VII:3, Fall 2015
Editor: Anna Faktorovich

Architecture of Being
By: Bruce Colbert

The Encyclopedic Philosophy of Michel Serres
By: Keith Moser

Forever Gentleman
By: Roland Colton

Janet Yellen
By: Marie Bussing-Burks

Diseases, Disorders, and Diagnoses of Historical Individuals
By: William J. Maloney

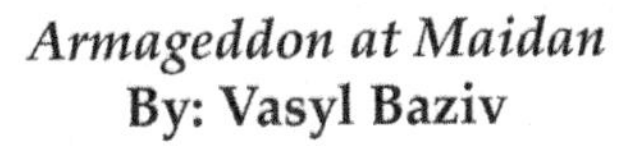

Armageddon at Maidan
By: Vasyl Baziv

Vovochka
By: Alexander J. Motyl

CPSIA information can be obtained
at www.ICGtesting.com
Printed in the USA
BVOW10s0849050817
491149BV00002B/151/P